Part of Ann Major's thrilling
CHILDREN OF DESTINY Trilogy!

The Bedroom Was Wrapped In Total Darkness...

...and he was darkness, too. For the first time in Dawn's life, she was unafraid, because Kirk was with her, because she was discovering that there was a beauty in darkness that could never be found anywhere else, a beauty in touching, a beauty in listening to the hushed wordless sounds of love, a beauty in the closeness of two bodies coming together.

Never had she been handled with such exquisite tenderness as she was by this hard, yet gentle, man.

"Kirk," she whispered. "I—I don't know how."

His fingers slid across her skin, barely touching her, yet arousing her until she was breathless. His lips caressed her throat, letting the sensuality that existed between them say what was so difficult to put into words. "Honey...Honey..." he whispered. "You were born knowing. You were made for this. I don't know how I'll ever get enough of you."

After a lifetime without love, she had found it. Only to know that it couldn't last.

He was the wrong man.

She was the wrong woman.

But neither of them would ever want another....

Dear Reader:

Welcome! You hold in your hand a Silhouette Desire—your ticket to a whole new world of reading pleasure.

A Silhouette Desire is a sensuous, contemporary romance about passions, problems and the ultimate power of love. It is about today's woman—intelligent, successful, giving—but it is also the story of a romance between two people who are strong enough to follow their own individual paths, yet strong enough to compromise, as well.

These books are written by, for and about every woman that you are—wife, mother, sister, lover, daughter, career woman. A Silhouette Desire heroine must face the same challenges, achieve the same successes, in her story as you do in your own life.

The Silhouette reader is not afraid to enjoy herself. She knows when to take things seriously and when to indulge in a fantasy world. With six books a month, Silhouette Desire strives to meet her many moods, but each book is always a compelling love story.

Make a commitment to romance—go wild with Silhouette Desire!

Best,

Isabel Swift
Senior Editor & Editorial Coordinator

ANN MAJOR
Night Child

Silhouette Desire

Published by Silhouette Books New York

America's Publisher of Contemporary Romance

To Diane Gafford—
for being one of the most
beautiful people I've ever known.

SILHOUETTE BOOKS
300 East 42nd St., New York, N.Y. 10017

ISBN: 0-373-05457-2

First Silhouette Books printing November 1988

A Note from Ann Major:

What matters to me are the cherished people in my life—most of all my husband and my three children. When I conceived my Children of Destiny Trilogy, the thoughts of family and love were uppermost in my mind.

I was born and raised in south Texas, and I've always loved our vast, desolate lands that seem to stretch forever beneath blue skies. I grew up on stories of the legendary men who carved dynastic empires out of desert, men who fought Indians and bandits.

Passion's Child, *Destiny's Child* and *Night Child* tell the stories of the Jacksons and MacKays, two such pioneer ranching families whose lives were intertwined for one hundred years by friendship, greed, betrayal and, ultimately, love.

CHILDREN OF DESTINY

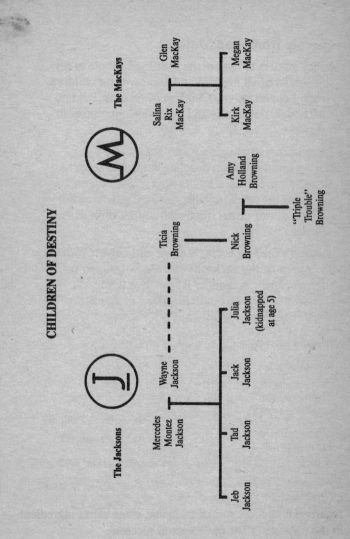

The Jacksons

The MacKays

Mercedes Montez Jackson — Wayne Jackson - - - - - - Ticia Browning

Jeb Jackson

Tad Jackson

Jack Jackson

Julia Jackson (kidnapped at age 5)

Nick Browning — Amy Holland Browning

"Triple Trouble" Browning

Salina Rix MacKay — Glen MacKay

Kirk MacKay

Megan MacKay

Prologue

The sky was flat gray, the washed-out color of old zinc. The trees were bare and dead looking; the windows shut against the cold. It was a day like any other of the season, a day without the slightest warning that the familiar pattern of her life was about to change, abruptly, completely, irrevocably, forever.

Dawn Hayden's toe shoes banged against oak flooring.

She wore a white leotard and tights. A gold medallion in the shape of a tiny sun flashed at her throat. It was the only piece of jewelry she ever wore. Where it had come from, who might have given it to her, she did not know. She only knew that of all the things she possessed, the necklace was the most precious. She never took it off—even when she performed. Lincoln had objected at first, but even he now regarded it as some sort of talisman, some secret ingredient in the formula of her phenomenal success.

A cold northern light filled the studio and blazed from the cool glass mirrors. Dawn's long black hair was down, soft and caressing against her exquisite neck. She was dancing alone to the crashing discord of rippling piano notes, her shapely legs whirling in a series of endless turns. Other girls in layers of sweaters and leg warmers were lined against the wall, watching her in a state of breathless awe.

No one in the company danced as Dawn danced. No one was like her. No one worked as hard, sacrificed as much for her art. In the studio she worked until she dropped. On stage she was an electric presence. The night before when she had danced *Ondine*, she'd received numerous curtain calls. Her dressing room had been packed with telegrams and flowers.

Dawn Hayden was Lincoln Wilde's darling.

There was magic in her dancing. When she danced, one had the feeling in the pit of one's stomach that something momentous was happening. Even during rehearsals.

But not a single one of the girls envied her.

Because she had no life, none at all, outside the theater.

"Miss Hayden is the ice princess of dance," one critic had exclaimed, and the label had stuck.

The studio door slammed, and the piano music faltered and then stopped abruptly as a tall golden man in a black turtleneck and slacks strode inside the huge studio and propped himself onto a stool dead center. All the girls sat up a little straighter and cast smiles in Lincoln Wilde's direction, hoping to catch his attention. But he frowned, cocked his head back, crossed his legs and watched Dawn.

Dawn stopped dancing and glared at him for a long moment. Then she limped toward him on her bad ankle.

"So," Lincoln murmured, "the rumors are true. You've gone behind my back and learned my new ballet when I told you I would never give it to you. Who taught you those steps?"

Blazing dark eyes met his, and as always he was struck by her intense charisma. She was a small woman, her bone structure as fragile and delicate as a bird's, and yet she was a creature of infinite grace and loveliness. A power in his theater, on stage and off. She was white skinned, black haired, long necked. Not so different from the other ballerinas and yet completely different. When she danced, she was incomparable. Lincoln had lived his adult life surrounded by beautiful young women, all vying for his favor, but even he had been irresistibly drawn to her ever since she'd come to his ballet school as a lonely child on a scholarship and had thrown herself into ballet with such energy.

She was perspiring, and she whipped the heavy mass of her hair forward over her shoulder and let it tumble loosely over her gently heaving bosom to her waist.

"I watched you showing Marguerite," she said, leaning down and picking up a white sweatshirt.

"You waste your time, and your time belongs to me. You should have been rehearsing for the gala."

One of the girls along the wall hiccuped. There were nervous giggles. These battles between the artistic director and his ballerina were common. With an impatient gesture of his hand Lincoln dismissed the other girls, and they quickly fled. The pianist grabbed her sheet music and scurried after them.

"They scare so easily," Dawn murmured dryly, yanking her sweatshirt over her head.

"And you constantly rebel," he whispered fiercely. "You do so in front of the others to incite them, I think."

She lifted her chin. Her hand touched her necklace and then fell away. "You constantly hold me back."

"Because I, not you, am the artistic director here. I know what you can do better than you do."

"I'm not a child any longer. I can't accept that."

"You never come to my class."

She would not look at him. "I have found my own teacher."

"That broken-down Russian windbag, Princess Sonya. She hasn't danced a leading role in twenty years."

"Sonya was the greatest dancer who ever lived."

"She was only on top for six years."

"Which underscores the problem." Dawn sat down and pulled on her leg warmers. "A dancer's life is short. I'm running out of time."

"You're a child. Twenty-five. You have years and years—"

"I have nothing except ballet." She stood up once more. "Do you understand? Nothing. You go home to a wife. I go home to a cat that doesn't even come when I call him. When I can no longer dance everything will be over for me. I will have nothing. You will have some new, younger ballerina. Marguerite, perhaps. You're wasting my time. Lincoln, unless you give me the role of Beauty, I'm leaving the company."

He was thunderstruck. "What?"

"Just for a while. To dance abroad. Then I want to go to Ali Naid and dance for that goodwill troupe to raise money for those people starving in—"

"Hell no!"

"You've given me your last order, Lincoln."

"Damn it! Why don't you take a lover like the other girls? That's what's wrong with you!"

Her eyes darkened. "You would think that!"

She turned and walked out of the room.

One

From the highest box in the domed theater a lone sharp-shooter in black robes and a flowing dark *kaffiyeh* watched the glittering ballerina through the cross hairs of his scope.

The girl swirled, leapt, seemed to hang suspended in the air, only to land light as gossamer on the brilliantly lit stage. Aslam Nouri squinted over his rifle as he struggled to follow her flight downstage. His cold black eyes gleaming with the predatory thrill of a fanatic, he zeroed in on Aurora's sparkling tiara, her pink satin, pink tulle and gold glitter. On the medallion at her throat. There! If he squeezed the trigger, his bullet would find her heart.

His finger twitched, vibrating with his impatience. It was not time. Not yet. And the girl with the golden coronet was not his target.

She was dancing the finale to the trombones in Act One of *The Sleeping Beauty*, Tchaikovsky's decadent Russian work, which would have no place in the new world Aslam

and his followers envisioned. Having just pricked her finger on the spindle, she was spinning wilder and wilder with
the pain to the mad presto of Carabosse's theme.

The girl began a dazzling feat of seemingly endless *fouetté*
turns. Five thousand Arabs sprang to their feet, and the
thunder of their applause swept the theater. The assassin
grimaced, set down his rifle and stole a swift impatient
glance at his watch. Then his eyes flicked to the darkest re-
gions of the balcony where he thought he detected the
shadowy forms of his men and the faint glint of light off a
gun barrel.

The constant bursts of applause were throwing all his
careful calculations off, but it was almost time. The music
began to build. His finger tightened as he waited for the
cymbals.

He lifted his rifle again, but this time it was not the fragile girl, but Prince Ali and his cabinet in the royal box that
he studied.

Despite his lavish uniform, Prince Ali was a coarse, arrogant man with coal-black hair and a thick curving mus-
tache who'd begun life as a peasant. His dark eyes were
deep-set and slightly bulging.

Aslam would have known that cold face anywhere, even
if it weren't emblazoned in every public square. It was the
face that had haunted his nightmares for more than a de-
cade. It was the face of the man who had ridden into Aslam's village, a small peaceful place on a barren slope dotted
with mud huts. It was the face of the one who had obliterated his boyhood, who had rounded up every man, woman
and child and shot them in the back of the head—Aslam's
mother, his sisters, his only little brother.

Hatred washed over Aslam in a thick, blinding red wave.
The cymbals crashed. Now! He rubbed his eyes, but it didn't
help. He couldn't see through the scarlet haze of his fury.

He pulled the trigger anyway.

On stage the hag Carabosse threw back her hood and cackled with evil laughter. In the prince's box, the bullet slammed a man in uniform backward. Aslam screamed with agony and frustration. The wrong man! He had shot the wrong man!

In the royal box, blood was everywhere. A chair was overturned as a man in a resplendent uniform leapt to the stage. Other men in uniforms were running, shouting. Panicked, Aslam dashed from his box. The prince was escaping.

On stage, four costumed princes unsheathed their swords and fell upon the evil witch, but in a burst of flame and smoke, she suddenly vanished. Aurora was placed on a litter as the real prince ran past them. There was a tremendous crash on the tam-tam and ffff chords from the brass. A rising mist seeped upward, veiling everything.

On her litter, above the fog of swirling vapors, as she was borne solemnly aloft offstage, Dawn's heart pounded from the exertion of her recent dancing. Her body and costume were drenched with sweat. Her tightly wound black hair felt loose, as if she'd lost half her pins during those dizzying turns and it was about to come down. A prong of her tiara cut into her scalp. and her right ankle cramped with the old pain. She needed an ice pack and a drink of water. Only she couldn't drink the water here because Lincoln had warned her not to until she got back to New York. He hadn't wanted her to come here at all. Lincoln always thought he was an authority on everything, and he had said this tiny Arab kingdom was too unstable. It had been delicious fun to thwart him for once and promise to dance the benefit. What did Lincoln know of Arabs? They had loved her.

Suddenly there were shouts. The music stopped abruptly at the crack of gunfire. Her litter careened madly, and she felt her body toppling even as she grappled wildly for something to hang on to.

Her injured foot hit the wooden floor first, and she screamed. But brown arms caught her, breaking her fall, saving her fragile ankle. She was about to thank her rescuer when his brutal hands cut into her flesh.

"You're hurting—"

A hand clamped over her mouth, smearing her lipstick.

"I will kill you, pretty American girl," the man whispered into her ear in an accent so terrible, in a tone so vicious and filled with hatred, it was amazing she could understand him.

She stared up into blazing obsidian eyes, into a face, cold with maniacal hatred.

"Stand you still," he ordered.

She understood every garbled word.

She felt the icy barrel of a gun against her hot perspiring skin. His long nose curved like an Arabic dagger above sensual-cruel lips. His savage features were those of a barbarian. If she lived a hundred years, she would never, never forget his face.

"Please," she begged, her own voice a broken rasp she no longer recognized.

Those merciless black eyes glittered above that dagger nose, and he smiled faintly, if one could call that menacing twist of his cruel lips a smile. He could slice her to pieces and relish doing so. His hand tightened around her throat, and he squeezed so hard she almost lost consciousness. The edges of the golden pendant she always wore dug into her neck, and a trickle of blood slithered in a greasily glimmering rivulet down her pale throat. Then he dragged her across the stage as if she were a sack of sand, shouting in Arabic, holding his gun to her head, using her slim stumbling body as a shield so he could escape. Her tulle skirt snagged on something and tore.

Desperately she twisted her head and stared at him again. Then it happened.

His dark face blazed at the center of fire.

Fresh terror engulfed her.

Cruel features whitened and blurred fleetingly into another equally cruel face from a long-forgotten past before vanishing altogether in the mists of her mind.

Afterward she would remember that image, and it would inspire terror. She would think of it again and again during those long days and endless nights in that filthy stinking cell the Arab would throw her in, but she would not be able to understand.

Her mind flooded with dazzling light, a blinding whiteness brighter than a million stage lights that obliterated everything. She could see nothing, but she was terrified. And she knew that this was an old fear. She had felt this utter helplessness, this utter aloneness, this terrifying sense of loss somewhere, sometime before. It was so terrible she'd never wanted to know that kind of fear again.

In a flash she knew that it was this secret fear at the bottom of her soul that drove her. This was why she worked so hard, why she had no life, why she danced.

She began to tremble.

"No! It can't be happening again! I won't let it!"

Her voice was choked with tears. She didn't even know what her words meant.

"No!" she cried.

She was frantic to escape this man who provoked such terror.

His hands were manacles of iron. She was powerless to move.

The old nameless fear was welling up.

Someone was shouting, shaking her. She heard her own voice, shrill and unrecognizable, louder than all the rest of the pandemonium.

Brutal fingers ground her windpipe into the bone, and she was silenced. She fell back, limp in the Arab's arms, and he bundled her up, running with her, carrying her outside into the smothering furnacelike heat of the desert.

Inside the cozy living room of a huge red-roofed mansion on one of the biggest ranching empires in all of Texas, Jeb Jackson was holding his fiery-haired baby son proudly in his arms. Jared made loud guzzling noises as he sucked voraciously at the rubber nipple.

"Don't feed him so fast," Megan instructed softly.

It was amazing how often it took the two of them to tend Jared properly. They were like a surgical team, hovering anxiously, ministering to the baby's slightest need as if these routine activities were of mammoth importance.

Jeb tried to pull the bottle away, but Jared only sucked all the harder with a frantic determination.

"Honey, he's a Jackson and a real Texan cowboy. He's not about to let a woman boss him."

"He's only six weeks old! Don't tell me he's already a lost cause—like his father!"

Male black eyes locked with defiant green ones, but as he studied his wife, Jeb's expression softened. This woman had filled his nights with passion, his days with excitement and happiness, and now she had given him a son. "He's old enough to go after what he wants." Jeb reached out and fingered a strand of Megan's red hair. It pleased him that it was the exact shade of his son's, just as it pleased him that every time she looked at him her face was transformed with love and gentleness.

Once she had fought him. Now she was his. Forever.

Across the room Jeb's parents, Mercedes and Wayne Jackson, were watching the news as they sipped cocktails. As always, Megan's brother, Kirk MacKay, stood apart from the others, wrapped in his own brooding silence, a lone wolf apart from the pack. Tall and swarthy, dressed in tight jeans and a black shirt that was slashed at the throat and hugged his lean body, he towered behind the older Jacksons. Every muscle in his body felt taut, caged in. He had accepted the dinner invitation only because Megan had begged him to.

Kirk turned his back on the television, bent his powerful body over the bar and poured himself a bourbon on the rocks. A brown hand restlessly swirled the crystal glass, but he did not bring it to his lips.

A young maid in a black-and-white uniform came into the vast room and cast slanting flirtatious eyes in his direction. Kirk looked up from his drink. He had danced with her at a country-and-western dance last weekend. He remembered her pressing her body into his; just as he remembered the hot invitation in her eyes. All his life women had chased him. He smiled faintly, cynically, and she blushed to the roots of her hair at his attention, barely managing to announce dinner in a tiny faltering voice before stumbling from the room.

Mercedes arose to switch off the television, but just as she did, the commentator started talking about the latest kidnapping in the Middle East. Mercedes' hand hovered on the button.

"Leave it on," Kirk commanded. His attention was caught, rapt, as was Mercedes'.

"And now our latest on the Dawn Hayden abduction in Ali Naid, tiny oil sheikhdom of Prince Ali Hufaz. Miss Hayden is a principal dancer for the New National Theater of Dance and Ballet in New York City, and at twenty-five, she is one of America's prima ballerinas. On the night before last, Miss Hayden had just finished the finale of the first act of *The Sleeping Beauty* for one of Prince Ali's gala charity events when seven gunmen interrupted her mesmerizing performance and attempted to assassinate Prince Ali. Though the attempt failed, one of the prince's top aides, Mussa Assad, suffered chest wounds and is in critical condition. Miss Hayden was kidnapped by the alleged leader of the band of terrorists as he was escaping. There has been no word of Miss Hayden in over thirty-six hours, and all efforts to locate her have failed thus far."

A color photograph of the dancer flashed across the screen. She was dark, slim, graceful, with the long-necked, ethereal beauty so common to ballerinas. Her pale face was a delicate oval. High black brows winged above enormous shining dark eyes. Her smile radiated warmth. She had an unruly mane of thick, ebony hair that cascaded over her shoulders in wrinkled waves. Even in that still picture, there was something wild, something vitally, irrepressibly and eagerly alive about her, something undisciplined and unruly that had no place in the face of a classical dancer. Hers was no polished, emotionless cameo. She was a maverick, and it showed.

Kirk found himself unaccountably drawn to the girl. There was a haunting vulnerability about her. He wondered where she was, what was happening to her.

He slammed his glass on the gleaming bar, and everyone turned to look at him. He flushed darkly. "Sorry."

They knew too well his dislike of kidnappings and terrorism, respected his privacy and turned their attention back to the television.

Acid chewed a bitter path through him as he thought of that slim pale woman brutalized and murdered by rough terrorist bandits. Kirk's green eyes, so like his sister's, hardened. It was better not to think of the girl. With an effort, he forced himself to relax. It wasn't as if he knew her, as if he could do something about her, as if it was his fault— this time.

"Too bad they got her," he muttered grimly. "She's probably dead by now. If she's lucky." He bolted his bourbon and poured another.

"Dear God!" Mercedes bit into her knuckles. A former dancer herself in her youth, she was always interested in any story however remotely connected to the ballet world. She had been following this one closely.

"Damn fool idiot!" Kirk muttered. "Girls like her don't have any business over there in the first place. Prince Ali is a brutal and total dictator, and many factions in his country have sworn to kill him."

As the news story unfolded, only Mercedes and Kirk remained to watch. There were more photographs of the girl and a clipping of her dancing *Ondine*.

Transfixed Mercedes watched. "Her dancing isn't perfect, but it is wonderful. Really beautiful. I once knew someone else, who danced *Ondine* almost exactly like that! My sister Anna..." Mercedes shivered and moved closer to the television set. Unconsciously her hand had lifted to her heart. "No..." Her voice was low, strangled. "It can't be..."

Kirk rushed to her side. Mercedes was as white as if she'd seen a ghost. He looked back at the swirling dancer. There was a strange sensation of impending doom in the center of his gut.

An enlargement of a pendant Dawn Hayden always wore blazed across the television screen. It was a tiny golden sun.

Mercedes' eyes widened. She made a little sound, and Kirk was suddenly afraid she was having a heart attack. She gripped Kirk's hand as she studied the pendant and whispered, "Julia! My baby!" Her wild eyes pierced Kirk's, but she wasn't seeing him. "Julia's alive!" she murmured faintly. "She's alive! They didn't kill her!"

Jeb and Wayne came running just as she collapsed in Kirk's arms crying, "Julia, Julia... Kirk, you have to save her. You have to!"

His face gray with alarm, Wayne tried to pull his wife from Kirk and cradle her in his arms. "Darling. Julia was kidnapped twenty years ago. She's dead. She has to be—"

Mercedes grasped Kirk's lapels and struggled to hang on to him. "No... that's her... A mother knows. The Longoria necklace... It's the same."

Wayne was smoothing the waves of her hair. "A coincidence, my darling."

"It's exactly the same as the one she was wearing the day she was lost."

Wayne lifted his worried gaze to Kirk, but Kirk was no longer aware of either of them. His immense muscled body was bent low over the television. He was listening to the commentator, avidly studying the pictures of the ballerina.

That tingling feeling was back in his gut, and Kirk had learned early in his career never to ignore it. Again and again it had proved to be the heartstring of his destiny. In his business, a man lived or died by hunches, by some inner sixth sense that had nothing to do with reason.

Kirk's mind reeled. *Julia!* Was it possible? After all these years?

Julia Jackson, Wayne's and Mercedes' only daughter, had only been five when she was kidnapped.

The girl's coloring was right, and she was the right age. She was a great dancer. Mercedes had been one of the best in the world before she'd given up her career to marry Wayne. Anna Montez, Mercedes' sister, had been a renowned ballerina. It could all be coincidence, and yet Kirk believed in coincidences and in things like a mother's intuition.

Mercedes was not a hysterical woman.

Until this moment, he had always believed Julia was dead. It was his fault she had been lost. He had been teaching her to ride at the Jackson stables when the men had come and taken her. He'd only been fifteen, but he'd fought like a demon to save her. In the end, they had beaten him senseless, and yet for a time the police had considered Kirk an accomplice and even gone so far as to lock him up.

The Jackson tragedy had haunted Kirk all his life. He had blamed himself. He had joined the marines to run away from the guilt, to make himself so tough he could handle himself in any situation. He'd even been in the CIA for a while. Since he'd come back to the ranch, he had rescued dozens of kidnap victims both at home and abroad, and every time he'd saved someone, it had been Julia he was saving. Only it hadn't been her, and the nightmares had always come back to haunt him.

It was his fault she had been lost. His fault.

The line of Kirk's lips was taut and white as he regarded another clip of Dawn Hayden dancing. His green eyes were slitted. In the golden lamplight his mother's Comanche blood showed in the high cheekbones that were highlighted where the skin stretched tightly over his hawk nose and beneath the hollows of his eyes. His was a harsh face, its dark handsomeness aged beyond his thirty-five years by the bitter experiences of his life.

If that girl wasn't Dawn Hayden, if there was even a chance she really was Julia Jackson, he had to go after her.

Damn! He didn't want to go. He must be getting soft. Lately life had almost been pleasant, now that Megan had settled down into a happy marriage with Jeb, now that he had his nephew Jared to be interested in. Kirk had had enough of the Middle East and its brutality to last him forever.

Images and impressions bombarded him. Latticed windows, goats, camel's thorn, women swathed in black, sandstorms, winding crowded streets, bazaars, thick black coffee, perfect blue skies above the golden petrified geometry of the desert. Always there was the dry scorching heat, the grit of sand in his mouth, his eyes, his nose. And the danger.

And camels. He hated those foul-natured, humpbacked miscreations.

Ali Naid! He hated the country as well. It was a country simmering on the verge of revolution, a nation filled with different factions of medieval-minded fanatics, all of whom hated each other with warlike ferocity, although they hated Westerners even more fiercely. It would be suicide to go in there alone.

Suicide to go up against a band of armed terrorists.

Two

——

A man's high-pitched wail rent the silence. It was followed by rifle bursts hitting something soft, then ricocheting against stone. Afterward silence filled the well-dark blackness with suffocating nothingness.

The stench of death and decay rose from the mattress and made Dawn's empty stomach give a dry heave. Terrified, she jumped off her filthy pallet and listened to the silence. *Dear Lord! Let this be a nightmare! Let me wake up!*

But as her torn nails dug into the mud wall, and she swallowed queasily and felt her tongue rub against the grit in her mouth, she knew this grim reality was no nightmare. Her injured right ankle was twice the size of her other one, and the pain every time she limped was excruciating. How many times had she awakened with the same fervent prayer on her parched lips? Always there was only this dank, putrid cell with its filthy pallet and windowless walls.

She licked her chapped lips. Her hand went to her throat, and she touched her medallion. She longed for water. In her sleep she even dreamed of it, but her jailer never brought water. Instead he brought the most awful coffee she had ever tasted. It was so strong, it tore her insides apart, but she drank it anyway because it was liquid and she was dying of thirst. Once he had brought her a hot, sweet bottled drink, and she had guzzled it greedily until every drop was gone.

She stared into the utter blackness and imagined that it must be the middle of the night. She had lost count of the days and nights. All she knew was that it wasn't as hot now as it was sometimes, especially during the day when the cell was most like an oven and a grayish brightness seeped in through the cracks in the door.

Everyone but Dawn was sleeping on the roof to escape the heat, but she had been locked in a cellar that was hot and still, and so dark that she sometimes felt the darkness lying like a heavy crushing weight on her chest.

Outside she heard a sound. As she listened she could distinguish the shuffling of heavy footsteps coming down the stairs, moving down the hall, the fumbling for the right key. She knew all the familiar sounds of him by heart.

The handsome Arab with the daggerlike nose and cold black eyes was coming. A scream bubbled up her dry throat.

The door opened. He set his flickering oil lamp down beside her food and seized her. She was blinded momentarily by the light. Black shadows danced eerily against the squat walls.

"Shut up, pretty American girl, or my men will come."

Her scream froze in her throat as the odd menace in his low tone sank in. Aslam always came. Only him. Suddenly she knew why.

When she quieted he let her go, shrugged and turned to leave.

"Let me out. Let me walk outside at least. I can't stand it in here."

He ignored her and unlocked the door again to go.

"Don't leave me in the dark. Please. No..." Dawn cried. He continued to ignore her, but in desperation, she pounced on him, grabbing his back.

He whirled around, his face distorted and savage. "I think you stupid, pretty American girl." His rough hands bit bruisingly into her forearms. He pulled out a pistol and shoved it against her head. She heard the trigger click.

His hands were shaking. Her face went as white as paste. In the flickering light, her eyes were as immense and dark as glimmering, hand-blown English marbles. Against her ear he murmured something in Arabic and began to laugh. As he reached to extinguish the lamp her fear mushroomed. All her life she had been terrified of two things—the dark and horses.

Now in the darkness he was laughing at her. "Tomorrow, you will die...like the others."

For years she had run from the real world. She had danced, the beauty she created on stage the only reality she wanted. In one shattering moment, her world had become too real.

So, this brute was not so different from his men. He was going to kill her. Tomorrow. Strangely, just knowing what her fate was to be made her fear lessen. A desolate, numbing peace settled upon her.

He towered between her and the open door, her only avenue to freedom. She considered her chances of getting past him, and they seemed infinitesimal.

But he was going to kill her, anyway.

As a dancer, she knew all about human bodies, their strengths, their frailties. In a single leap she jammed her good foot hard onto his instep. He pitched sideways. Her nails found his eyes, her knee his crotch.

He doubled over with a groan, and she picked up the lamp and banged him over the head. Then she broke free and hobbled down the hall on her injured ankle.

She was running up the stairs when a tall shadowy figure loomed out of a corner. A hand coiled from the darkness, and she was caught and knocked breathless against the tallest, hardest male body she'd ever felt. Her breasts were pressed against corded chest muscle; her thighs ground against his.

Her first captor had been big, but he seemed as nothing compared to this man. A rough, callused hand covered her soft mouth and strangled her scream.

As he pushed her deeper into the darkness, she felt the terror tugging at her, making her markedly conscious of how slight and fragile her body was compared to his. He jammed her against the wall with his powerful torso and twisted her face so that a single bar of moonlight from a high, narrow window slanted across it.

Though he brought his face close to hers, she couldn't see him. His hard features were shrouded in darkness, but she could feel his gaze burning across her face, studying her, no doubt assessing her charms. Was he going to take her for himself? Or share her with the rest of his friends on the roof? Suddenly the four walls of her cell seemed a paradise when she thought of being used by this brutal stranger and his cohorts.

Rough fingers trailed the length of her throat. He lifted the medallion and held it for a long moment. Then he sifted through her hair, holding it to the light as well. During this intense inspection of her face and necklace and hair, she could feel her heart pounding, her breasts pushing against his chest. He was holding her so intimately that it was impossible not to know the exact moment when his maleness reacted to the feminine nearness of her helpless body. Panicking, she twisted, and her body rubbed itself even more tightly against him in that most intimate of places. She felt the warmth of him, the size of him. Too late, she froze.

She could feel his lips curl in mockery at her modesty. Some taunting guttural sound came from his throat. He let her hair fall like a veil over her shoulder.

There was no way she could stop him from doing whatever he intended, but she held herself rigid, raising her chin in helpless defiance, and stared hard at him, her black eyes crying her fear and hatred of him.

To her amazement, when she stilled he relaxed his grip on her mouth, and the minute he did she bit his hand so hard, she tasted the bitter metallic flavor of his blood.

"Bitch!"

She was so caught up in struggling to free herself from him that she didn't notice he had spoken in English, and that his perfect pronunciation of the insult was American. She lurched past him, stumbled down the stairs, limped the length of the hall and fell full force against Aslam.

"You see there is no escape, pretty American girl," Aslam said grimly, grabbing her by the throat.

She thought he knew of the stranger on the stairs. "Why don't you bullies just shoot me, and get it over with?" she whispered.

"That would be too quick. Too easy." He touched her cheek briefly once, almost gently. "You should not have danced for Prince Ali, pretty American girl. It was big mistake. I have never killed a woman before. I do not like to kill you. You are brave—for a woman. But foolish, as all women are." He threw her roughly toward her prison.

He did not want to kill her, he said, but he would.

In the darkness of her cell, after he was gone, she closed her eyes, and the blackness seemed to suck her deeper and deeper. There was a blinding white flash and a stabbing pain in the back of her head. Only this time there were even more images that made no sense to her.

She was a child running lightly toward a boy who had an Indian-dark face, green eyes and straight black hair. He was holding out his arms, and she was filled with an inexplicable joy. From behind her, without warning, she heard the sound of thunder, only it wasn't thunder. It was a man on a demon-horse, the pounding of its hooves shaking the earth as man and horse bore down on her. Frightened, she turned back to the boy with the green eyes, but he had disappeared. Just as she was fainting with terror beneath the flying hooves, a hand clamped around her waist, pulling her up, slinging her belly down across the saddle. The last thing she saw was the mad gallop of horse's hooves, the careening ground, flying rocks.

Slowly Dawn came back to the present, but her courage had melted before this vision. Every nerve-ending in her body was vibrating with fear. Was she losing her mind? Was it the perpetual darkness? Was that why she was having these terrifying white flashes? She'd never been able to stand the darkness.

She collapsed on her filthy pallet. Whether it was hours or minutes later, she would never know. Something heavy thudded against the wall outside, arousing her from her terrified lethargy. She sat up and strained to hear. Someone or something fell hard again. There was a muffled cry of pain as fist slammed into bone. A boot heel into gut. A desperate battle was going on out in the hall. She heard a single shriek of agony and recognized that it belonged to Aslam.

He had come back.

Why?

Was it time for her to die?

There was an ominous quiet, but she knew someone was outside the door.

Quickly she shoveled everything, her food, the lamp, her scanty belongings under the ragged quilt and ran to hide behind the door.

A key turned in the lock, and she shrank against the wall as the door opened a crack. In the gray-black light she made out the glint of a gun barrel. Then she saw the immense outline of a masculine body.

It was the menacing stranger from the hall.

He was death's angel, and in an instant flash, she knew she was not ready to die.

He stepped into the room and approached the bed, speaking softly, almost beguilingly. He had come to kill her. She knew it.

He pointed his gun at the lump and kicked it. When it remained motionless he snatched the quilt aside.

She bolted outside, only to stumble over a slumped figure in the doorway and fall flat on her face on the dirt floor. Behind her she heard the merciless clamor of footsteps as the giant tracked her. She struggled to get up, but she was weakened from her imprisonment. As she crawled along the floor, the man lunged and dragged her back by the hair, falling on top of her, rolling with her. When they were still, he pinioned both her wrists above her head, with one hand. Straddling her waist with his thighs, he held her down. All she could do was kick and flail the air helplessly with her legs. Still she fought him, twisting in his hold, her soft body like a sweet devouring flame wherever any part of him touched her.

In breathless English, he whispered, "Honey, don't make me hurt you."

Through the haze of her terror, his words made no impression. Aslam had spoken English, too. She kept struggling, so he tightened his grip. Her arms went numb.

She felt the warm grizzle of the man's unshaven cheek against her face. She heard his ragged whisper, "Julia, honey...it's Kirk. Don't fight me."

Names from the past.... They meant nothing.

Memories assailed her and were gone, vanishing into a mist of whiteness and terror. Kirk... Julia... What did they mean? Who did they belong to, these names? The flashes of light? They had to do with nightmares. Her head throbbed dully.

All she knew was that this monster who held her down was some living figment from a long-forgotten nightmare that had been more horrible than even her present terror. He had said he would come back, and he had.

She struggled more fiercely than before.

"Damn," he muttered. "I didn't want to do this."

He wrapped a cord around her hands and bound them behind her back. Then he stuffed a wad of clothing into her dry mouth and gagged her. Her eyes flared with new hatred as he yanked her unceremoniously to her feet and pushed her forward. When she stumbled on her bad foot, he leaned over, examined it and uttered a low curse. When she cringed from his rough probing, he slung her over his shoulders as if her weight was nothing and stalked down the hall.

As he bore her up the stairs to a fate too horrible to contemplate, her tortured mind went mercifully black.

Three

Fiery waves of pain, radiating from Dawn's ankle, brought her whimpering back to consciousness. Her mouth was dry and sore from some hideous cloth that seemed to work like a dirty sponge, soaking up what little moisture had remained in her parched tissues. Thin cords cut into her wrists like knives.

The narrow room was hotter than the cell where she'd been imprisoned before, and it stank with some gagging smell from a dark smoke sifting through a glassless window. But at least the brilliant moonlight cast her surroundings in a silver half light, and she was no longer in the dark.

Then she saw him, the cause of all these new miseries, the malevolent giant who'd accosted her on the stairs. He was dressed in his long black robes with a black *kaffiyeh* draped rakishly over his head, its folds concealing his face. He was leaning his great male body nonchalantly against a wall as he shoved a cartridge into a long-barreled gun. He set the gun down for a second and took a lengthy swig from a goatskin jug.

She could hear the liquid sloshing in the jug as he drank from it carelessly, and her dry tongue flailed against the wad of cotton stuffed in her mouth.

He set the jug down and licked his lips. Even in the dim light, she could see a pearly droplet glisten on his mouth before he smeared it away with the back of a long-fingered brown hand. The lip of the jug glimmered with the same wetness.

Her thirst was like a dry ache in her sore mouth. She could feel it burning in every parched crack of her lips.

The swilling, thoughtless pig! She shivered with hatred.

He gave not a thought to her comfort, not a thought to the possibility of her thirst. She could be dead for all he cared. Instead, he turned his attention to his weapon. She didn't know anything about guns, but as she watched his deft movements, his nimble expertise, she knew he must surely be a professional killer.

Dawn felt a premonitory quiver at the base of her spine as she considered what he'd probably do to her. Then she fought to stifle the chill of fear. Son of the Devil, he might be, but he hadn't shot her yet. He hadn't even touched her. And he had something to drink.

She writhed and twisted, straining against her bonds until she hurt all over in an effort to attract his attention.

He was totally absorbed with his gun, rubbing it lovingly, loading it. She watched those long tapered fingers move up and down his weapon as gently as though he were caressing a woman.

When he did look up it was never at her. He kept a sharp eye on what was going on outside the window. There was a predatory silence about him, the careful, patient waiting silence of the hunter, the silence of a man in total control of his body and his emotions.

She was going to have to scoot herself across the dirt floor to get his attention. Very slowly, because of her ankle and her bound hands, she inched toward him, moving her feet forward, placing her hands on the ground, and then lifting her hips, repeating this slow, painful process over and over again.

Suddenly, in reflex to the unexpected motion in the dark room, he whirled. His gun clicked, and she was staring down the shiny black length of it into the steel slits of his narrowed eyes.

She squeezed her lids shut and gulped a deep breath.

He lowered his gun. Carefully he set it down and swaggered toward her, bending down to her level.

"So you're awake at last, sleeping princess?" His voice was smooth and soft, faintly mocking and so sensually pleasant that it made her shiver. "It's about time."

She nodded, furious that she could find any part of him attractive, even his voice. Then she bounced her trussed body up and down on the ground. A torrent of abuse welled in her soul and blazed from her eyes.

He pushed the folds of his *kaffiyeh* aside, and a sliver of dazzling desert moonlight cut across his harshly chiseled features. She found herself staring into the most beautiful pair of green eyes she had ever seen. They were densely shadowed by the longest, straightest black lashes that no man, let alone this brute, deserved. Every dancer she knew would have gladly sold her soul for such exquisite eyes and lashes. Yet there was nothing feminine about their hot male appraisal as they swept insolently from her face downward, lingering on her small breasts budding against her scanty pink costume.

She had always hated men who stripped women with devouring glances. She especially hated this one. There was something about his eyes, something dreadfully familiar that she didn't dare dwell upon because if she did, it would stir that vague, unnameable terror that came with those blinding white flashes and headaches.

"You look like hell," he murmured, bringing her back to the present with a torrent of abusive gibes, "but at least you're still in one piece. When you've had a bath, you won't be half-bad—for a skinny, bosomless runt."

Bosomless! Runt! Normally she would have bristled from such insults, but she was hopeful that maybe his thinking her less than perfectly endowed was what had thus far kept him from physically attacking her.

This hope was instantly dashed when the bloodied hand she had bitten moved toward her forehead. He meant only to smooth the limp black snarls out of her eyes, but she cringed, afraid of what any gentleness from a man like him might mean.

He read her terror and snapped his hand back as if burned, his expression grim. "I'm not going to hurt you, princess," he growled. "And as for wanting you in that way—" His voice lowered to a sneer. "You're not my type."

He spoke English! This fact finally penetrated. He spoke English! With some sort of twangy Southern drawl! He was an American! A despicable, insulting one, but an American.

He wasn't one of them! But if he wasn't, who was he?

She lifted her trembling chin, and through lowered lashes, she studied him warily. What she saw rekindled all her chilling fears.

He seemed half-tamed and lethal, his large body coiled with a savage inner tension. Smooth, sun-bronzed flesh stretched tightly across his prominent cheekbones, giving him the ruthless aura of an Indian warrior. There were hollows beneath his eyes and grooves etched into his cheeks. His hawklike nose had been broken once and never set.

He was older than she, by at least ten years. She could see the fine lines beneath his eyes as well as the deeper ones bracketing his mouth. A jagged white scar winged from his left black brow and disappeared inside his *kaffiyeh*. Someone hadn't liked him any better than she did and had split that bitter, arrogant face open.

He had lived a hard life, and it showed in the implacable set of his square jaw, in the thin determined line of his mouth, in the world-weary cynicism of his eyes. Not a trace of boyish softness lingered in his harsh features. He was all man, virile, terrifyingly masculine to the core. Obviously, he was an uncooperative, domineering sort. He hadn't shaved in days, and the shadow of thick black bristles intensified his thoroughly disreputable look.

She had always liked elegant, sophisticated men, not he-men, brute male chauvinists without an ounce of culture like this gorilla.

Her eyes glittered with disdain. He read her mind. When she frowned in distaste, his magnificent knowing eyes sparked with the faintest trace of insolence before he deliberately obliterated it.

She forced herself to look away as though she had grown bored with him.

Awareness of his tightly-coiled, awesome maleness consumed every pulsating sense in her body.

"I guess I don't look any better to you than you do to me," he drawled dryly. "Like it or not, we're stuck with each other, and believe me, I don't like spending my time with some sissy-girl in toe shoes any better than you like being with me."

She struggled, fought against her bonds, chewed on her gag in rage.

"Hey, hey," he whispered, grabbing her arms and holding her still. "When you think you can control your urge to scream like a shrew or attack me like a spoiled brat—" Her eyes riveted guiltily to his bitten hand. "I'll let you go. You damn near chomped off my thumb back there."

She hesitated, glaring at him sulkily, hating having to strike any bargain with such an odious individual, especially one who was responsible for her helplessness and gloating over the power he held over her.

"Look, lady, I've come through hell to try to get you out of this jam you so stupidly got yourself into."

Stupidly! What did this Neanderthal know of charitable deeds, of the sacrifices civilized people and entertainers made to help those less fortunate? She'd come here as part of an international goodwill troupe. The proceeds of the ballets she had danced were to be given to feed hungry children in Africa.

"Princess, do you have any idea of the danger you've put us in? We're right smack in the center of Aslam Nouri's terrorist camp in a remote village he controls. Worse, we're slap-dab in the middle of one of the world's most inhospitable deserts. I just beat the hell out of the guy and took his prime hostage. He's the most vengeful revolutionary fanatic this hellish country possesses. He would love nothing better than to rip out our hearts with his dagger and cook them over one of those wretched camel-dung fires that's stinking up this luxury suite. The only thing keeping us alive right now is an avaricious peasant I bribed into lending us this stable until daylight. If we get out, I've promised to make him a rich man until he dies. I'm your only hope, honey. Do I make myself clear?"

She stared at him in wide-eyed horror.

"Now, if I take off your gag and you make the slightest suspicious sound, we're both dead. And believe me, honey, these people have vengeful natures. They know how to make the most of a woman, even a skinny one, before they kill her."

He traced a callused fingertip from her lips, down the length of her throat, to the crest of her breast, his sensuous male touch saying more than ten thousand words.

His finger had burned a blazing trail down her skin. She shuddered, aware of him in a way she had no desire to be.

And he knew it!

His hand lingered for an infinitesimal second, near her nipple, heating her flesh, making her tremble. Something hot and dark and possessive flashed in his eyes. At last he pulled his hand away.

"So if you think you can squelch those murderous urges you feel toward me and keep quiet, I'll untie you," he muttered grimly. "Otherwise, I'll leave you like you are. Nod your head if you plan to behave."

She twisted her head up and down urgently.

When he hesitated, obviously reluctant to untie her, she bobbed it back and forth even more frantically. His eyes were skeptical, but at last he leaned over her and very gently untied her hands, her feet. Then her mouth.

She ran a bone-dry tongue across her crusted lips. "I'll despise you forever for the way you treated me, you...you, macho-man Neanderthal," she whispered, her low, ragged voice filled with loathing.

"If I'm so lucky," came his sardonic snort.

"What do you mean?"

"I just hope I've got—a forever. Then suit yourself, your highness." He shot her a leering grin. "Hate me."

All he was interested in was saving his own despicable hide.

She tried again to lick her lips with her dry tongue. "I'm thirsty," she whispered.

Casually he handed her his jug. She took one drink, wrinkled her nose, and wrenched the jug away from her lips with a grimace. "What is this stuff? I want water. Not this hot, putrid..."

"It's camel's milk, my high and mighty princess," he said with a smirk. "I sprinkled in a tad of bourbon to improve its flavor."

"I hate bourbon."

"I hate camel's milk. Drink it. The water here is even worse."

He got up and went back to the window. Satisfied that there was nothing to be alarmed about outside, he rummaged in his pack, pulled out a can, carefully peeled back the top and handed it to her.

Vienna sausage!

After the nauseous alien stuff she'd been fed, the mere scent was heavenly. She pulled a sausage out and sank her teeth into it. She had eaten at the best restaurants in New York, but nothing had ever tasted as luscious as that first tender pink sausage dissolving between tongue and teeth. She stared up at him, her dislike lessening, a fierce gratitude shining in her enormous eyes as she licked her fingers. She ate the rest of the sausages greedily.

"Drink the juice, too," he advised. When she had finished he squashed the empty can with his heel and put it back in his pack. Then he took out a sack and shook some dates into her palm. "Eat them slowly."

"Who are you?" she asked, when she'd finished the dates. "What are you doing here?"

He was holding his gun again, looking out the window, trying to ignore her.

"I asked you a question."

Something flared in his eyes, then vanished into the dark silence, and he said nothing.

"Didn't your mother ever teach you any manners, Mr. he-man?"

He turned his expression so dark and forbidding she cringed. "I never had a mother."

Unwittingly she had touched some ancient pain, one she understood too well. "I'm sorry," she murmured in a low, muffled tone.

"Do you think I give a damn for your apologies?" He stopped, clenched his jaw. "I liked you better gagged. Like most women, you talk too much."

His harsh words stung, as did his harsh demeanor. She lifted her head angrily. "If we're going to be stuck with each other, I just thought I ought to know something about you."

"There's no need," he replied tautly.

"Do you always get your way?"

"Most of the time," he gritted.

"I feel sorry for your wife then."

His mouth twisted cynically. "I'm not married."

"I can see why."

He practically threw his gun down and came toward her. His gaze was so hard and unfriendly, her bottom lip began to quiver. "Look, I need to concentrate on keeping us alive. If you'd just shut up, things would be a whole lot easier—for both of us."

"Maybe for you. Not for me," she whispered forlornly.

She needed to talk now that she was with someone, who, for all his obvious shortcomings, was actually on her side. It didn't matter on what subjects. For dozens of days and nights she'd been locked in that burning dark cell, with the terrifying Aslam her only companion, his constant threats of her imminent rape and murder her only conversation. She was half-starved, and she'd endured it all without a trace of hysteria. But now for some reason, now that she felt a bit safer with this man, her emotions were rising to the surface. She needed him to at least act like a human being instead of some macho-tough mercenary soldier.

"I bet you've never been scared in your whole life," she whispered.

He knelt beside her and took her raw wrists in his, turned them over and studied the bruises. Though he didn't say anything, she could feel his concern. With a finger he tilted her delicate chin to the light. He studied her smudged white face, the dark circles under her too-brilliant eyes. Briefly he touched her necklace. Then the black marks on her throat.

"Sure I've been scared," he admitted grimly. He knew all about being scared, all about growing up young and weak, fending for himself most of the time, all about people not thinking he or any MacKay was as good as the rest of folks, all about being locked up in a reform-school cell, hated by everyone, accused of kidnapping the child he'd nearly died trying to save. This girl was at the center of his life going wrong, but he didn't talk about those things, ever, to anyone. He'd learned a long time ago that people like this woman just wanted to pick and probe at him until they found out all the details and then despised him.

When he dropped her wrists abruptly, she caught one of his big brown hands in hers and pulled him back, liking the hot warmth that emanated from his skin to hers. His eyes reluctantly met hers again.

"At least tell me your name," she begged.

She wanted to know about him. She had to know about him to stave off some terrifying loneliness. He seemed locked up inside himself, remote, determined to be indifferent to her.

"I—I don't usually talk so much," she pleaded. "Really I don't. It's just that I was alone...so long...and so scared. Please tell me your name."

Her gaze fell to the silver identification bracelet he wore. Oddly there was no name. Just a figure of an Irish wolfhound engraved deeply into the metal. With a broken fingernail she traced the outline. She had the uncanny feeling she'd seen that bracelet somewhere before. Once she'd studied it with the same fascination she felt now. Her hand began to tremble.

Kirk hesitated, his expression stern as his stubborn will warred with the strange emotions she aroused in him. She seemed so young, so terrified, so vulnerable. Once he'd been like her.

Her hands squeezed his fingers. "Please...oh, please...Don't shut me out."

His eyes were steady as they probed hers. He saw her terror, her desperation, and something inside him softened.

He grimaced. He had a job to do. Any distraction could cost them their lives. He did not want to be moved by her, but he was.

"Kirk MacKay," he muttered in a grim low tone, "for what it's worth."

"K-Kirk..." Her voice was a thready whisper. "Kirk..."

She was aware of his eyes on her face, as though he were watching her intently to determine her reaction. When there was none, he relaxed.

The name made him less the mercenary, more human somehow. Her grip tightened on his work-toughened hand, the one she had bitten.

"I'm sorry I bit you," she said weakly. "I didn't realize..."

"I know."

She felt the cold metal of his bracelet pressing into her, the strength of him flowing from his flesh into hers, his awesome power, and as she held onto him, the hard masculine features of his face blurred in a blaze of white that filled the room.

She knew his face, the bracelet. From some nameless time and place—long ago when she'd been a child. She knew his eyes. But where? How? Why had she forgotten these things? Why did it hurt so much to remember them now?

There was a splintering spasm of pain at the base of her neck.

She recalled her earlier vision in the cell. She had been running toward a boy with green eyes and straight black hair.

She knew, though she didn't know how she knew, that this man, though he was older and harder, was the person she'd seen. Just as she knew—he was not her enemy. She had loved him.

What did it mean?

Why had he come for her?

She bit her cracked lips to keep from screaming. The world seemed to spin in a diamond-white caldron, and his haggard face was at the center of that whirl.

When the awful sensation passed, and she came back to the reality of a dark table and camel-dung smoke, she was shivering and weak with queasiness, drenched in her own perspiration. Kirk was holding her shaking body tightly in his arms.

Though the comfort he gave her was wordless, she had never felt so safe anywhere as she did wrapped in his silence, cradled close against his powerful, muscled body. It was as if she had come home after a long journey, as if she had been dead and miraculously brought back to life. The world seemed new, her senses sharper.

Her cheek rested against his shoulder. He was blistering hot, but she welcomed his heat. His rough hand was gently stroking her hair, loosening the matted tangles.

She didn't move or say anything because she was afraid if she did, he might let her go. And she never wanted him to let her go. She never wanted his fingers to stop combing through her hair.

He had come to this hellish place for one reason only—to save her.

Once they had belonged together. There would be time later, if they lived, to examine that. If she dared.

All of her adult life, she had lived without the touch of a man. She had lived only to dance, and her career had been meteoric. Dazzling and bewitching then on stage, she had been worshipped by every girl in the dance corps. It was as if a special magic was breathed into her soul when the stage lights were turned on, and only then could she truly live. Offstage, she was remote and withdrawn, her heart and soul empty of emotion.

Frederick, her last boyfriend, had complained. "You have nothing to give to a man. You are like a beautiful doll that's hollow inside! All your fire and passion is for the stage and an audience of strangers." So many men had been disappointed in her, and she had not cared.

Only Lincoln had been pleased. "You are lucky. You're meant for one thing only. Most artists live without this clear vision of who they are. If you work hard, I will make you the greatest dancer in the world." And he had. She had become a star, rushed through the night glimmer of crowded New York streets in white stretch limousines, feted at gala affairs.

For a woman like Dawn, there had been no suffering because there were no temptations. Other girls wanted to live, to have friends, to go to parties, to eat sumptuous meals at elegant restaurants. They had boyfriends, husbands, babies that meant the end of brilliant careers. Never Dawn. She had lived solely for the brilliant ballets Lincoln created for her.

Kirk's heat, his passion flowed into her slender body and transformed her.

It seemed she was awakening from a long dream.

Her mind wandered with a vague sense of déjà vu. She had danced this part a thousand times as Aurora in *The Sleeping Beauty*, and she knew every nuance of the role by heart.

In the ballet Aurora lay in a deep sleep on her canopied bed, her palace smothered with dark clouds and a tangle of undergrowth and weeds. Suddenly something hot and warm and alive pressed down upon her cold lips and breathed life into her. As she awakened in her Prince Charming's arms, the gloomy palace slowly filled with light. To the crash of cymbals and the rising tempo of Tchaikovsky's romantic music, the silent, motionless figures of court officials and servants began stirring to life after their hundred years' sleep. The overgrown weeds enveloping the room died down. Draperies of dusty cobwebs fell away, vanishing forever.

A prince's kiss, and the spell had been broken.

But this man and this moment were real and more wonderful than any finale to Act Two of *The Sleeping Beauty* could ever be.

In Kirk's arms, the familiar patterns of her lifetime were ended, and she was reborn into a new world where she was lost and uncertain. She would never feel she belonged anywhere else but with him.

His fingers touched the necklace she always wore, then lifted it so that he could examine it. Abruptly, as though burned, he let it fall back against her throat.

She had always been alone. Forever she had been waiting for this moment—when she would know that she belonged to someone else.

It no longer mattered who he was, where he'd come from, or who she was. Nor did it matter that they were strangers, that they came from disparate worlds. Some force more powerful than either of their individual wills drew them irrevocably together.

Gently he lifted her white face to his dark one, and she was powerless to resist him. His expression was odd, changed. The cold mask of his icy control had melted.

One glance into her luminous dark eyes, and he too was lost. All his anger toward her for having gotten him into this horrendous mess was gone, all his reticence toward her as a woman vanished. His harsh features slackened and grew softer. She touched his cheek, traced the slight curve of his nose and could not imagine why she had not seen from the first how devastatingly handsome he was. His green eyes flared. In their sharp spiraling flame, Dawn instantly recognized unbridled male desire.

He wanted her as she wanted him.

A thrilling breath caught in her throat. He touched her chin tenderly and drew her mouth to his. Every muscle in her body froze as searing male lips tentatively met the softness of hers.

Then bunching her thick black hair tightly against her nape with his fingers, Kirk kissed her as though he would die if he didn't, and the hot glorious response he evoked in her was new and frighteningly exquisite. With her hands she felt his body through the voluminous black robes, exploring the contours of his muscles, the bulging male shape of him.

He was shaking from her gentle touching, and though she'd never known passion in a man before, she sensed her heady power over him. With a soft moan she melted against him. His kisses sent ripples of fire sizzling from her mouth to the core of her being.

His tongue entered her mouth and traced its hollow warmth. Flooded with an eager shimmering yearning, Dawn let her head fall back, limp and compliant. One of his hands slid inside the ragged gilt-edged bodice of her costume and found her breast to trace its rounded softness. Her nipple crested, tightening against his rough palm.

She wanted his hands on her body—everywhere.

"I want you," she whispered, "to love me."

He drew a harsh ragged breath. It would be so easy to take her. He thought of her small firm body beneath his, pressing against him, and he went rigid with desire. She was looking at him in that hot way that made him know he had only to push her down, only to remove her torn costume, only to touch her naked flesh to have her quivering beneath his hand. He wanted to kiss her until her mouth became soft and sweet against his, until little whimpers rose from her throat. He wanted to make love to her until she begged him to take her, until she shuddered and moaned in ecstasy beneath him.

This woman was a stranger.

And yet she was not.

He had never desired a woman more.

Outside there was a shout. Men were running toward the stable, their boots and guns clattering past it, and Kirk MacKay was sprawled helplessly on the floor about to make love to the woman he'd come to rescue.

Had he gone mad? How in the name of hell had he let things go so far? How could he have forgotten that they were in the middle of Aslam Nouri's armed camp?

These realizations brought him fumbling back to his senses. He raked his hand out of her costume and shoved her away. His heart was pounding violently. His face was flushed, his breath heavy, and he bent his head to keep from looking at her.

"Why... did you stop?" she whispered shakily, dazed with hurt and rejection.

Her voice was sweet as honey, flowing into him. Never had anything or anyone been more precious to him.

He wanted to pull her into his arms, to take her then and there.

He got to his feet and stumbled like a blind man toward the window.

Outside three men were chasing a donkey that had gotten loose.

Kirk turned back to her. "Don't you understand? Anyone could have come in here, found us, slit our throats."

She heard only his harshness, his coldness. "B-but..."

"If you're smart, you'll leave me the hell alone." His voice was rasping, unsteady. He picked up his gun and checked it again. "What happened to the girl who was going to hate me forever? You certainly changed your tune in a hell of a hurry."

"*You* kissed me!"

"My mistake, sister!"

"Oooo! I hate you!"

"Good!"

She turned away and buried her face in her hands.

If only she did hate him! At least then she might salvage some remnant of pride left to her. But no! She had been so starved for human companionship, she had practically thrown herself at him.

What kind of man kissed a woman so tenderly as he had, as though he were crazed for her, and then brutally rejected her? A tortured sob rose in her throat.

From the window he broodingly watched her miserable figure. Her head was bowed so that he couldn't see her face, but despite the concealing dark waves of hair spilling over her shoulders, he knew she was crying. He had hurt her, and he hated himself for making her so unhappy.

"Look. I'm sorry, okay?" he mumbled gruffly. "I'm not mad at you. I came here to save you, not to get you killed. I shouldn't have let myself forget where we were." His voice softened. "Why don't you lie down and get some rest? Tomorrow's going to be a long day. We're clearing out of this dump as soon as the sun comes up. It's going to be 120 degrees by ten o'clock. Moon's going down right now. That means daylight in about two hours."

It wasn't the world's most gallant apology, but to her it seemed so. She wiped her cheeks dry of tears. "Why don't we go tonight?"

"Because your friend Aslam and his men are lurking behind every mulberry tree and mud hut," he said.

"And won't they be able to find us better in broad daylight?"

"Not if we're invisible."

"Have you lost your mind?"

The grooves beside his thin lips deepened. "Trust me."

"That's not so easy, you know."

He squatted against the wall under the window and laid his head back wearily. Suddenly she realized how tired he was.

"Lie down," he said.

This time she obeyed, but with the light of the moon gone and Kirk's forbidding silence, the blackness seemed stifling, choking, worse even than when she'd been in that cell. Her fear of the dark was like a ripple from a thrown stone in the middle of a pool. It started in the center of her being and spread until it encompassed every part of her. She covered her lips with her hand, not wanting him to hear her when she began to whimper.

But he heard. "What's the matter now?"

"Nothing..." But she couldn't check the low sob that strangled even the tail of that single word.

"There damn sure is. Either tell me or shut up. I'm trying to sleep."

"You don't understand."

"Try me."

"I—I'm scared of the dark."

Scared of the dark and she'd come to a country on the verge of revolution! "It figures," he muttered sarcastically. He wished he could ignore this crazy woman and her shivering sobs, but somehow every snivel seemed to tear his heart out. "Come over here, then," he muttered roughly.

"No. You don't want me."

"That's true, but I'm dead tired, and neither of us is going to get any sleep if you keep this up. Swallow your pride and get over here."

She hated him for his smug superiority, for his courage in the face of grim danger.

She closed her eyes, and the dark seemed filled with demons and skulking Arabs with curved knives. Reluctantly she edged toward him. When she almost reached him she stopped, her pride holding her back, but he grabbed her by the hand and pulled her against his body. Even though she knew he despised her, his nearness made her feel safe, protected, and gradually the shudders of fear died as she nestled against him.

He was glad of the darkness, glad of any barrier between him and this fragile woman. The barriers of a lifetime of careful emotional control were crumbling, and he didn't want them to. He was safe when he kept his heart locked away. For years he'd avoided women, any real closeness to them. Still, she was a little thing, pleasant to hold. Dangerously pleasant.

He knew the exact minute when she fell asleep. Her head drooped on his shoulder, her lips touched the pulse beat of his throat. She was so close he could feel the whisper of every warm breath beneath his unshaven jaw, the tremble of her every heartbeat. Her scent enveloped him and it was sweet despite all she'd been through.

Almost unconsciously his hand came to rest on the curve of her hip and slid softly up her flat stomach. He marveled again at how tiny she was, how perfectly formed, even if her figure wasn't of the lush voluptuous variety he'd always preferred. His two hands could span her waist. She was built delicately with small bones like a bird, as though she were meant to soar. She was lovely just as she was.

Gently he brushed his lips against her hair, then her closed eyelids and pulled her closer. Though he hated admitting it even to himself, he wanted her beside him. Had she remained on the other side of the room, he would have ached to hold her in his arms.

It was dangerous to become involved with her, a danger to both of them.

But she was a comfort. Maybe his last.

Four

___

A fierce desert sun streamed through the window, dabbing the squalid walls with patches of brilliance. A stray red beam flashed across Dawn's face. Lazily she tried to twist out of its reach. Kirk grabbed her arm, and she stirred in annoyance.

She rubbed her eyes and yawned, slowly becoming aware of several unpleasant facts. There was a new stiffness in her neck because her head had rolled from his shoulder and lay crookedly against the hard wall. Her face and eyes were covered with grit. Worse, in the night she had become intimately entangled with Kirk's rock-hard body. His long black robes had ridden up, and to her horror she discovered that he was wearing almost nothing beneath them. Heat glued their clothes to their bodies, stuck bare skin to bare skin.

Her ankle was throbbing because a naked, hairy leg was sprawled on top of it. She blushed when she realized his hand was casually draped across her breast and his legs jammed tightly between her thighs. If they had been lovers, they could not have been more inseparably coiled.

Then the coldhearted brute jostled her arm again, and she jumped, furious.

"Time to get up, princess," he drawled in a huskily velvet male tone.

Warm fingers on her breast moved possessively, just a little, and she felt a tingling awareness from his touch.

She remembered the way he had so callously rejected her.

"Don't you dare shake me again!"

"Since you're awake now, there's obviously no need."

Her eyes focused on the harsh lines of his dark, unrepentant face. He had removed his *kaffiyeh*, and she saw that his hair was thick and black and cut ruthlessly short except for an errant lock that fell rakishly across his brow. Despite his dark growth of beard, he had the kind of bold dangerous beauty her ballerina friends would have found irresistible. Most scoundrels as good-looking as he, knew their appeal and made the most of it. All the beautiful men she knew in the dance world certainly did. They went from woman to woman.

He read her sour expression, knew she was thinking the worst of him, and he winked at her roguishly. "Do you always climb all over your lovers at night?"

"How dare you imply—"

"Oh, I wasn't implying," he replied cheerily. "You don't leave a man alone. Why, at one point you climbed on top of me and even touched . . ."

He seemed quite pleased by these events. A horrified breath caught in her throat as she realized that one of her hands was at that very moment still curled inside his naked thigh. She yanked it away.

"W-would you shut up!" she stammered, shaken. "You don't know when to keep quiet."

She heard his low chuckle. "Neither do you."

His bold hot eyes were devouring her. It was obvious he thought her a man-hungry wanton. Her cheeks flamed. "I never... I mean not once..." She broke off helplessly. Oh, Lord. What was the use of trying to make him believe she didn't sleep around?

"It was damned hard to sleep," he murmured, "with you all over me." His hand on her breast moved ever so slightly again. "Besides that, you snore, princess."

"I do not!" she whispered in a burst of stung vanity. She shoved his hand and his leg away and flounced grumpily to her haunches.

He was studying the delectable curve of her spine and those rounded haunches intently. At least she wasn't skinny there. His warm amused eyes rose languidly to her face, and she found that even though she wanted to ignore him and try to recover her ravaged dignity, she could not look away from that insolent, jewel-dark gaze.

Those glorious eyes held her spellbound, stripping her, probing to her very soul. She felt the heat of him, the dangerous wildness pulsing just below the surface. Sleeping with her had stirred him. She who had lived such a disciplined, circumspect life had never known man-woman wildness before this moment, had never wanted to know it. But it was coursing through her veins now, as he cast those devouring liquid eyes on her. She sensed the extraordinary depth of his male sensuality, the extraordinary depth of the female sensuality she had never known she possessed until he had so effortlessly aroused it in her. She began to tremble, not just from fear but from her utter helplessness to deal with this new inexplicable susceptibility.

"You do too snore," he taunted, but his voice had softened and was almost tender. "Just a little." Feeling her shiver, he drew her back into the circle of his arms because he was too hot-blooded to resist doing so. "I guess all your lovers have been too gallant to tell you that. You should try sleeping on your stomach. I've heard it helps."

"For your information, I know I don't snore, and I'm not promiscuous the way a scoundrel like you probably is. And... I—I don't even have one lover. I've never..."

She felt his muscles tense as he brought her closer, staring into her eyes. She could feel his heart pounding where her fingers grazed his chest.

His emerald eyes touched her mouth and the jutting swell of her breasts with a suggestive look that sent the blood rushing to her cheeks again.

"I thought all dancers in New York City," he murmured, "especially famous ones... took lovers."

His nearness, his eyes, the heat of him, the shared intimacies of the night, the expert fingertips that traced a line along her throat, that sensual low voice of his, all these things, intensified her discomfiture.

"Well, you thought wrong!" she said, stumbling over the words.

"Not that it matters—to me," he replied casually, "how many you've slept with... or haven't." She stiffened with hurt even as she felt the strong grip of his hands harden possessively on her arms, pulling her closer, belying his indifference.

She closed her eyes, wishing she had more pride than to let him draw her once more into his arms. Thus, she didn't see him gazing down at her soft frightened face framed by the flowing wildness of ebony waves, his desperate expression that of a man who knew he was lost despite his powerful will.

It was with pleasured surprise that she felt his hard mouth caress her temples, his breath warm against her skin. When his lips met the solitary tear that glazed one eyelash, he tenderly kissed it away.

His fingers curved along her slender throat, turning her face toward his. She held her breath, not daring to breathe for fear his lips would cease exploring her. When his mouth closed over her parted lips, she could taste the faint saltiness of that single tear he had kissed.

She sighed in utter surrender, but as her fingers curled into the silken thickness of his ink-black hair, Kirk ripped himself from her, placing his hands on her arms, his iron muscles keeping his body apart from hers.

She opened her eyes dazedly and met the fury of midnight-dark eyes blazing from beneath the thick fall of black hair that tumbled across his brow.

"Kirk?" She murmured his name in startled confusion.

His chiseled features were a carved bronzed mask. Hers were soft and flushed with desire.

He tore his gaze from the trusting innocence of her beautiful face.

"Don't hate me," she whispered brokenly. "Please . . ."

A muscle twitched in his jaw. "If only I could, princess," he breathed out roughly. "If only I could."

A chill ran down her spine. She felt caught in a vacuum of boundless despair.

He kept looking at her, his eyes burning fiercely, his heart pounding just as fiercely. Slowly he got a grip on his dark mood and pulled her to her feet.

"Look out the window," he commanded.

Outside the village was coming to life. Men were strolling out of their tents and huts in answer to the call for prayer. Aslam Nouri was drawing an arc in the sand with the end of a glinting saber while his men knelt before him, all of them facing toward Mecca.

The mere sight of the dark Arab made Dawn cringe closer to Kirk. She couldn't take her eyes off the dagger-curved nose, the cruel lips of her former captor. She scarcely saw the other armed men taking their ritual splashes of cleansing water, going through the motion by sprinkling sand over their shoulders. She was too terrified to hear the ancient chant when it began, *"Allah akbar, Allah akbar . . ."* God is great, God is great.

Her face was white with shock and fear. She was remembering Aslam's hands on her throat and thinking that if he found them, he'd kill them and relish doing so, and tomorrow he would pray again at dawn. Her hands circled Kirk's lean rangy waist, and she clung to him with a long racking shudder.

His anger forgotten, Kirk edged his body closer to hers and lowered his chin to the top of her head, hoping he could comfort her by his proximity. He felt her slender body quivering against his. Poor woman, she was scared to death. She kept seeking closeness with him; he kept pushing her away. She didn't snore; he'd merely said that to annoy her.

He felt a twinge of pity for her. She was only a woman and hardly more than a child, at that. There were black bruises on her throat and arms where that bully had brutalized her. Never before had she known the terrors of war, of murder, of death. He thought her almost courageous when he considered that.

On the whole he'd never had much use for women. It was part of the reason he distrusted the powerful feelings she aroused in him with just a look, a word, a touch. In his experience, women were trouble-makers, the lot of them. Hadn't his mother, whom he'd adored, run off and left him without so much as a goodbye when he was just a kid? She'd broken his heart and taught him that no female could ever be trusted. His father hadn't been much good at anything after she'd gone, either. What with his old man's gambling and drinking, the family had ended up with nothing but a few scrap acres of their once sizeable ranch. Then his father had gambled even that away. Their family pride had been obliterated. Kirk's baby sister, Megan, had grown up half-wild, and if ever there were a female born to get herself into jams he was supposed to bail her out of, it was Megan. Luckily she'd finally married Jeb Jackson, and it was Jeb's problem to tame her now.

Kirk had become sufficient unto himself years ago. He didn't need a woman, didn't want one...for anything except the obvious. Unfortunately he was too sexual, and the need tormented him with an awful regularity. Because of this weakness, he had fallen in love once or twice and gotten his heart smashed all over again. He was through with women and the games they played, through with closeness and tenderness and emotional pain. This woman might seem different than the rest, but she wasn't.

Inside the houses, the women said their prayers silently.

Soon the chanting ended. A boy began rhythmically pounding freshly roasted coffee beans, the stone pestle hitting the side of the brass mortar like the clapper of a bell. The women came out of the houses to rekindle the previous night's fires by throwing twigs from desert bushes and dried camel dung on the embers.

Kirk groaned. "I hate camels. More than anything, I hate camels," he muttered, puckering his nose, as the thick acrid smoke curled toward them. "I'd rather smell a ripe skunk on a hot Texas highway, anytime. Let's eat breakfast while we can still breathe."

Breakfast was spare—a few dates, more of the terrible camel's milk laced with bourbon, and two thin slabs of stale, unleavened bread. When they finished eating Dawn was still hungry, but she didn't complain. He was bigger than she was and probably hungrier, too.

"Clean everything up," Kirk ordered briskly. "A date seed in the dirt could mean the difference between life and death."

Quietly she obeyed, but when she opened his satchel to put the seeds inside, she drew back astonished. The satchel bulged with an arsenal of guns, knives, wires and dynamite, but what startled her was the money. Stacks of neatly bound one-hundred-dollar bills were crammed into the bag.

"Where did you get all this money?" came her breathless question.

He looked up from his gun. "I was sent over here with a million dollars to negotiate your release," he said tersely.

"Who sent you?"

Silence.

She picked up a packet of bills and thumbed through them. "You didn't even try to negotiate."

"Sure I did." His savage gaze glittered briefly. "I negotiated with that Nouri bastard last night outside your cell when I kicked him in the guts." Kirk tucked a gun into his belt. "I'm negotiating now."

Her knuckles were white from the death grip on the wad of bills. What was going on? "By just taking me out in some stupid macho way, one man against hundreds. Who do you think you are, Rambo? If you'd talked to them, maybe they would have just let me go."

"Yeah, maybe," he agreed, his own temper flaring. "But in case you haven't got things figured out, it's way too late for that now, princess."

"Oh, that's great! Just great! We'll probably both die because of your stupidity."

He shot her a derisive look. "Because of yours, sister. Neither one of us would be here at all if you and your pretty pink toe shoes had stayed in New York where they belonged.''

''I bet you didn't talk to them because you just wanted to keep all that money for yourself. You probably don't even care if I get killed or not—so long as you get to keep the money.''

Low, harsh laughter came from his throat, but his eyes were bright pools of anger as he stared at her, his face so hard and bitter that she shifted uncomfortably. ''Oh, that's good,'' he whispered roughly. ''That's good. Just what I need—a woman who reads me like a book. Get dressed, princess.'' He tossed her a black bundle and a pair of sandals. ''No more time for chitchat. We're leaving.''

''Now?'' Her eyes rounded with fear. ''You can't mean we're just going to walk out—you, me and a million dollars, when they're all outside. Aslam Nouri—''

''Now!'' he ordered.

She fumbled with the bolt of black cloth, spilling it to the dirt floor. ''What is this thing, anyway? What are you putting on?''

He was dropping a black tentlike dress that completely covered his head and body. Within seconds even the slits for his eyes were almost veiled.

''This is the veil,'' he said, ''known in different countries by different terms—the *abeya*, the *chador* . . . Originally it was designed to protect the modesty of Arab women. Lucky for us, the custom still prevails here.''

''You mean, we're simply going to walk out . . .''

''No man would dare molest the honor of women under Aslam Nouri's protection,'' he murmured, with an acidic touch of irony.

She pulled the black fabric over her head and adjusted it so she could see out the slits.

"Believe me," Kirk said, "through the centuries, men have often worn the veil for all sorts of dubious purposes— to get into harems, for assignations. If it gets us out of this jam, I for one will always be one hundred percent for the custom."

"And have you ever used it to get into a harem or get close to an Arab girl?"

There was an awkward silence, and she suspected that he had.

"You're awfully tall and long legged for an Arab woman," she said dubiously, as he towered over her. "I'm surprised they didn't find you out and cut you to ribbons."

"So I'm good at mincing with my knees bent."

"I never would have guessed you were a man whose talents lay in that direction."

"Only when my life depends on it." His patience was being stretched. She could hear it in his terse tone. "Ready, princess?"

He handed her a basket filled with coarse shirts and hand spindles and skeins of yarn to complete her disguise so that she would seem like a Bedouin woman on her way to sell handmade goods in the bazaar.

A shiver of apprehension raced icily over her flesh. No, she wasn't ready to go out there among all those terrorists with nothing but a thin, black bit of cloth to protect her! But as she watched Kirk stuff his satchel into a woven basket and retreat toward the rear of the stable, she dashed after him.

Outside she had to walk on her injured ankle without limping, but because she was a dancer, disciplined to perform with debilitating injuries whenever necessary, she did so with stoic valor. Because of their cumbersome veils, Kirk couldn't see that, after only a few steps, her lips went bloodless from pain.

Armed men, with cartridge belts laced across their chests, were everywhere. Every dark male face with a hooked nose brought back her terror and a forboding chill at the prospect of being recaptured.

Her teeth chattered with fear when Kirk made no attempt to avoid the most crowded part of the village. She could have gladly bashed him as he headed boldly for the thickest cluster of soldiers. With a flurry of flying feathers, chickens squawked and scattered before them as they walked along the dusty streets. There were donkeys and goats in the yards, the smell of roasting sheep, the scent of leafy vegetables aboil.

Men were hunkered down beside the small, adobe-colored houses shelling pistachios. Women in black, dressed exactly as Kirk and Dawn, scurried everywhere. From crude, tented stands, people were selling leather sandals and belts, trinkets, copper and pottery.

Kirk made his way through the bustling throng to a crowded fruitstand and began to bargain with the seller for two watermelons.

Watermelons! There were soldiers everywhere! Why was he stopping to bargain for watermelons?

If his mere stopping wasn't bad enough, he made it into a long drawn-out, nerve-racking process, thumping on melons, bickering over prices. All the time he haggled, Dawn's heart was pounding like a drum in her ears. Was his Arabic really as good as he obviously thought it was? Wouldn't the fruitseller notice how unusually low his voice was for a woman?

At one point Aslam Nouri passed within inches of them. When his black gaze lingered full on her face, burning through the black slits that concealed her eyes, she thought surely he would sense her terror, seize them and drag them to some hidden courtyard and murder them. But his gaze left her. He turned his back and vanished into the crowd.

She could have screamed with frustration when Kirk, having bought two, began thumping a third melon, holding it close to his ear. She had the feeling that he thrived on danger, that instead of being as terrified as she was, he was exhilarated. She wanted to use his head like the melon he kept thumping and give him a pounding he wouldn't forget.

At last he found a third melon that satisfied him, and after a lengthy exchange of verbal abuse he bought it. But he was not content to leave the market until their baskets were stuffed with melons, dates, hazelnuts and pistachio nuts. Only then did he head for the outskirts of the village, though he took a meandering route through the narrow streets, veering always toward the east, where a formidable eternity of bleak, barren country with hardly a bush or a tree stretched endlessly. There were canyons with deep caves, but they, too, were as barren as the open country.

At the edge of the village, they came to a deserted hut. Behind the house a rangy, lazy-looking young bull camel was tied to a stake.

Kirk ripped off his veil and cloak and stuffed them in his satchel, cursing roundly. "That rotten, lying cheat! May that stinking Arab suffer blindness and be boiled in oil."

"What's wrong?"

"Just look at that miserable animal! I paid a hundred *sukki* for him."

The camel's long lashes flicked nastily at Kirk, as man and beast regarded one another with a mutual lack of regard.

"He doesn't look so bad—for a camel."

"I was promised three. And twice as many water bags. But never mind. We've got to get the hell out of here, and he's all we've got."

Quickly Kirk donned a white *kaffiyeh* with a black cord and the loose attire of a poor Arab. Then he picked up the camel stick leaning against the hut. Dawn started to take off her own veil, but Kirk stopped her.

"No. Stay as you are. We'll look like a poor Bedouin and his wife on our way across the desert.

Rivulets of sweat ran down her face and her spine as the black cloth drew in the heat of the burning sun. Her leg throbbed from her ankle to her knee, and she felt faint from the heat and hunger, and from the long walk after having been locked up so long, but she made no complaint.

Kirk took the camel stick and walked over to the beast, yanking the nose rope and beating the beast in an effort to make the animal kneel. The camel stretched his neck viciously and tried to take a bite out of Kirk's arm.

Kirk ducked and turned back to her, snarling softly, "Hey, you two will probably get along just fine. You've both got the same instincts."

The remark stung, but she lowered her head and tried to ignore it.

At last, kicking and spitting, the camel knelt in the sand. "Come on over here and get on him," Kirk commanded.

"Get on him?" The camel, who appeared in the foulest of moods, was glaring at her from between the slits of its three pairs of lashes and making ghastly snorts. "You have to be out of your mind!"

Kirk was tying their baskets and jugs and satchel onto the glowering camel while the beast whined loudly. He was hanging goatskin water bags to the saddle. "I said get over here!" he yelled. She didn't move an inch. "So help me if you don't, I'll tie you on his back."

She moved warily to his side, and before she could argue further Kirk lifted her up and heaved her into the stiffest, most uncomfortable seat she'd ever been in. "Honey, this is going to be heaven compared to trying to walk across the desert on that ankle."

The camel whined even louder at this fresh load and swayed back and forth in an effort to dislodge her. "Kirk!" she shrieked.

"Hang on, princess."

When she managed to do so the beast spit nastily in Kirk's direction.

"I don't think he likes me," she whispered weakly.

Kirk wrestled the reluctant beast to his feet. "Princess, he loves you. He's unusually affectionate for a camel."

The camel's lips parted; his head swiveled toward Kirk again, but Kirk hit him with his stick. "Save your strength for the desert, lover boy."

Kirk's eyes studied the burning desolation of shifting sand dunes that stretched toward the horizon.

To try to cross it during the heat of the day with only one camel, with a weak and injured woman, without adequate food and water was suicide.

Kirk knew the desert, and he was afraid, as all intelligent men were afraid of it; even the Arabs who wandered through the desert and knew it better than anyone.

He had only a sextant, only the sun and the stars and a hand compass to guide him. The slightest mistake in navigation could make him miss the vital well he was heading for. A half a mile, either way, would be fatal.

One camel. And not a very good one.

He'd seen perfectly healthy-looking camels drop after a day or two in the desert.

Then the woman would die. Of thirst.
He did not want to watch that, but he would.
Then he would die last of all.

Five

It was the evening of their third day in the desert, and the sun was sinking. Kirk was too exhausted to feel gladdened that the terrible heat of the afternoon would soon by dying. He could feel nothing but bitter despair as he watched the clouds billowing on the horizon as the desert cooled.

Three days. They had long since eaten the melons, the nuts, the dates, his rations, almost everything, and their water bags were nearly empty. The sides of his stomach ground together incessantly, but he was long past feeling hunger pains. Dawn was so weak that Kirk had had to tie her to the saddle, and her slumped, unconscious body dangled precariously to one side. He was having to pull harder and harder at the nose rope to prod the camel onward.

But Kirk plodded on, determined, despite the terror that lurked just beneath the calm surface of his disciplined self-control. He would rather die walking than lie down in the sand and give up. They should have come to the wellhead hours ago by his calculations. Still, he refused to admit his failure. He kept clinging to the desperate hope that they were moving so slowly that his timing was off.

The sun drooped like an obscene, fiery flower, its trailing petals brushing the edges of the earth before wilting altogether. The sky purpled, and a brilliant moon rose quietly.

All desert moons and desert suns were bright, and desert skies were the most beautiful on earth. But Kirk was too dead with weariness to appreciate their beauty. Though he knew he could not walk all night, he would not let himself think of stopping, or giving up.

Over the next rise, he kept promising himself. *Just another quarter of a mile, and we'll be there. Over the next rise... water...*

The camel climbed a small hillock of drifting sand, stared across the empty desert that seemed to stretch to eternity and collapsed slowly on his haunches. No matter how frantically Kirk pulled on the nose rope, no matter how loud he shouted or how hard he beat him with the stick, the animal refused to budge. The camel merely eyed him indifferently.

Finally Kirk went to Dawn, pulled out his razor-sharp knife and slit her bonds. It never occurred to him to leave her. He slung his satchel filled with money over his shoulder. Then he lifted her into his arms and continued to trudge through the sand. He was almost over the third rise when he stumbled and fell, collapsing breathlessly into the sand and rocks, too exhausted to rise. He knew with the sinking inexorable knowledge of a man facing imminent death, that he had pitted himself against the desert and lost.

It was only a matter of time before the last of their water would be gone.

Lying in the sand next to the woman, he closed his eyes. He immediately sank into a deep sleep. When he awoke, he heard voices, laughter. He sat up, thinking he had dreamed them, that his desperate mind was playing a cruel trick on him. But as he listened, he made out distinct words of the desert tongue. Never before had he dreamed in Arabic.

A fragile hope flared. He knew that in the open desert, sounds could travel a long way, but he got up and dragged himself, crawling by inches, to the top of the hill, hardly feeling the camel's thorn and rock tearing at the flesh of his hands and knees.

Beneath him a tiny flame licked a star-sprinkled sky.

This was no dream.

The well! They had reached it! There were twenty tents. Hobbled camels grazed on clumps of thorn. Azid, his Bedouin friend, had set up an encampment as he had promised.

Kirk went back to Dawn, wearily scooped her up and walked down the hill toward the oasis.

The grazing animals became restless, sensing a stranger. A tall man lifted the fold of a tent, squinted into the darkness, gave a shout that brought other men, and then ran forward. One shocked glance into Kirk's haggard face, and the Arab took the girl into his own strong arms.

"When you did not come yesterday, we thought you were dead, my friend," he said in the ancient tongue of the desert.

Kirk's lips curled, but he couldn't manage a smile. He tried to speak and couldn't manage that, either. Instead he pitched crazily downward into the sand, unconscious, fainting for the first time in his life.

It was cool inside the tent. Kirk dipped the rag into the jeweled bowl and washed Dawn's pale face, let the liquid trickle into her hair and sponged her neck with its yellowing bruises, her shoulders and her breasts, trying not to think of how alluringly soft and lovely she was.

All it had taken to revive him was Azid dashing water into his face, a roasted leg of lamb that he had gnawed voraciously until the bone gleamed in the moonlight, a long drink, a sponge bath, a shave and two hours' rest. Then he had awakened, his first concern for Dawn. He had stormed into the women's section of Azid's tent and found Azid's women gently ministering to her. They had bathed her and washed her hair in water sweetened with frankincense, rubbing her body in perfumed oils. They had spooned water between her still lips.

When Kirk discovered that she was still unconscious and burning with fever, he had insisted on taking over the task of caring for her and had shooed the women from the tent. There had been startled gasps from the women as they'd quickly covered their faces when he'd entered, shy giggles and chattering as they left. A man could die for daring to break the sacred taboo of entering the private quarters of another man's women.

Kirk heard Azid's low voice from the other side of the dividing cloth, excusing the rudeness, "Wife, my friend has been away a long time. He forgets our ways. He is half-mad from the desert."

With swift efficiency Kirk had stripped away the white robe the women had dressed Dawn in. Then with hardly a glance toward her naked body, he had bundled her thick perfumed hair above her head so she would be cooler.

He had forced tea and broth, a little at a time, down her parched throat and sponged her body repeatedly. When at last, after hours of this labor, she seemed cooler and her naked skin glowed from his frequent spongings, he lay down beside her, gazing into her thin, pale, beautiful face.

How still her thick lashes lay against the gray pallor of her cheeks, he thought. How dark were the blue-tinged shadows beneath her eyes.

He felt a funny constriction in his heart. She was such a little thing, and she had been incredibly brave, scarcely complaining these past few days. Never once had she pleaded for water or food or rest.

Every night she had slept snuggled against him in his arms, and he had wanted her there.

Julia... Darling Julia. He had found her at last. If only she would live, the tragedy that had haunted him for a lifetime would be over. He could bury the guilt, forget the little girl who'd been stolen while in his care and go on with his life.

For an instant he remembered the child she had been. She had been a rowdy, sparkling and adventurous little girl with frizzy black hair and enormous dark eyes, the adored only daughter of the immensely wealthy Jacksons. There were those who had said that she'd been born with all of the Jacksons' most deplorable characteristics. She was demanding, stubborn, willful, and yet in this tiny imperious creature, everyone found those traits enchanting.

Kirk had always had a softness for children and treated them gently, and Julia had loved him, tottering after him the minute she'd crawled out of the cradle. With him, there had always been adventure. Mercedes had trusted her with him, had let him take her up on his horse. When Julia was five she had demanded her own mount. "I want a horse, Mommy, so I can be a cowboy and ride with Kirk."

"Cowgirl, *querida*."

"No! Cowboy! Just like Kirk!"

It had not been long before the Jacksons had granted this most fervent wish of their darling child. She was given boots, chaps and a cowboy hat. Then a small intricately carved saddle studded in silver. But she had cried she wanted nothing but a horse.

Kirk had led her outside and shown her her new pony. The next day he had begun teaching her to ride. Because there was not much love in his life, teaching her had quickly become one of his favorite pastimes when he'd gotten in from school and finished his chores.

Then on that fateful afternoon when Mercedes and Wayne had been away, three men had ridden into the paddock. At first Kirk had thought they were cowboys coming in from the range. When he realized they weren't, they already had Julia. He'd told them to let her go, but they'd laughed in his face. "You think you're tough enough to stop us, kid? We'll show you tough."

One had grabbed him, binding his arms behind his back, while the other beat him until he was senseless. Then they left him for dead in the dirt and had galloped away with the screaming little girl to a pickup truck they'd concealed in the dense cover of a mesquite-shaded ravine.

Kirk had been blamed by everyone and locked up in a cell with a dozen juvenile delinquents for that hellish time. Yet no one had hated him more thoroughly than he had hated himself. His own guilt had torn him apart. Every night for years he had burst violently awake in a cold sweat with the vivid memory of Julia's tortured screams.

Because of him, a precious little girl had wanted to learn to ride. Because of him, she was gone.

The ransom had been paid, but the child was never found.

For years everyone except Mercedes had believed she was dead.

Dawn shuddered delicately. Kirk's eyes remained glued to her still face.

"Julia..." The name was a velvet whisper in the darkness. It was an agonized masculine sound filled with hope and a terrible yearning.

Briefly he touched her fevered brow.

It seemed he had spent his whole life determined to find her, to save her. He was damned if he was going to watch her die now.

There was nothing more he could do for her except to let her sleep, and he was feeling tired again himself.

He'd never been one to wear much to bed, so he tore off his hot desert robes and lay down beside her. Then he draped his arm protectively across her waist, hoping that she would sense his presence. He fell asleep with his body curving against her warmth.

It was the middle of the night. A deep breath swelled against the planes of his muscled chest. A soft velvet weight was crushing him in the darkness. But it was not unpleasant, not unpleasant at all.

If only it were.

He came awake slowly to the languid coil of satiny arms and legs enticingly entwined with his, to the engaging sweetness of Dawn's innocent face pressed closely to his, to the feel of naked breasts snug against his chest.

God, she felt soft, even lush. So innocent and yet so bold. A fluid dissolving heat flowed in his veins.

She had climbed on top of him again as she had that first night when she'd been afraid, and he'd taken her in his arms. Only this time she was naked, and his own chest and legs were bare. Only this time he was less wary of her because he was growing used to her. He was in a camp with armed friends, and instead of a stable wall and dirt floor, they were lying on soft, comfortable Bedouin carpets beneath cotton covers and blankets.

Her delicate hand was curled trustingly around his brown neck. Her head lay gently nested in the cradle of his shoulder, her black hair sweeping his arms like skeins of perfumed silk.

He supposed he was getting accustomed to her ways, to her craving for physical closeness because now he wanted her near him all the time. His fingers drifted down the length of her spine, over the curve of her buttocks, and he realized that she was perspiring. Her skin was cool. During the night her fever had broken.

He sighed, happy that she was better, even as he hated the sudden hot surge of his maleness that made him want to forget all that she had been through and just roll over and take her.

It would be so easy to slide his legs between hers. So easy to...

"Damn!" The ragged whisper exploded from his lips. Then he let out a sigh heavy with self-disgust. How could he be such an animal when she was weak and defenseless? Though he hated to move her, he didn't trust himself to go on holding her with her body locked so tightly to his.

Carefully he slipped an arm beneath her head and tried to nudge it onto a nearby pillow. He was sliding her body from his, when she moaned softly, and her hands clutched him, clinging gently.

"Hold me," she whispered drowsily in her sleep. "Just hold me."

She nuzzled her face against his clean-shaven cheek, touched his throat with her lips, and he cursed himself for the fiery shaft of desire her kiss instantly caused.

He had sought a child and found a woman. He could have handled a child. The woman seemed bent on handling him, at least, when she was nearly unconscious.

His heart thudded wildly. She lit a fire in him—body and soul. It was agony to hold her and not take her, but, for her sake, he forced himself to endure it.

He stared quietly at her for a long moment, but the fine, delicate beauty of her face merely intensified his torture. Her

inky lashes lay against her fair, flawless skin, and he remembered the dark iridescent loveliness of those captivat-
ingly slanting eyes. How they had flashed their dislike of
him when she'd been gagged and bound, and later, how
they'd heated with warmth after she'd let him kiss her.

She amused him. She angered him. She entranced him.
She was awakening tender feelings he'd kept suppressed so
long he'd forgotten he'd ever felt them.

Smooth and gleaming faintly with oil, Dawn's mouth was
curved into a gentle smile, as though she were very content
to lie in his arms, as though she had no reason not to feel
safe and protected there. Her long black hair streamed in
soft waves over his arms. He wound his fingers in the jet
strands, liking the way they slid across his skin.

She was lovely, and he knew his need for her was growing with every day that passed. It shouldn't be happening.
He didn't want it to, but in some mysterious way she was
setting her hooks into some deep part of him. Maybe that
was just because he'd never known a woman anything like
her. Maybe it was simply that he hadn't taken her yet.

She adjusted her body to his, moaning ever so softly in
her sleep. Her fingers brushed the dark fur of his chest,
tickling him. Then the tiny hand stopped and curled around
his waist and awakened every nerve ending in his belly.

Soft fingertips curved into the inside of his navel and
made a hot quiver of desire dart through him. His body
went rigid, and he balled his hands into fists, jammed them
against his sides and stared straight up into the darkness,
terrified of losing control.

She slid her leg across his thigh and made a sound like a
contented purr. She was soft as velvet, and she made him
feel as hot as flames.

This night was both heaven and hell, and Kirk wanted it
to end. He wanted her to wake up. He wanted an end to this

hot, steamy flow of his emotions and desire. But her body felt infinitely sweet pressed into his. He hadn't slept with a woman in a long time. He had forgotten how good it could feel.

He wanted to hold her forever, even if he died with longing.

She had said she was a virgin, and as he lay wideawake in the darkness, savoring the full rounded softness of her breasts against his chest, he considered that. For all his experience, he had never taken a virgin.

Suddenly he knew that when she was better, before he took her home to New York and Mercedes, he was not going to be able to stop himself from having her.

She would be his first virgin.

He would be her first man.

An even trade.

The world famous ballerina and the Texas cowboy. His mouth twisted cynically. Never before had his taste run to fancy things. Nor to fancy women with tastes for fancy things.

She was not his kind of woman. He knew it in his bones. No matter how much they were attracted to one another here where they were far from their own lives, inevitably they would part and return to their own worlds. She was a city girl, used to living in that insane beehive called New York City where brilliance mingled with mediocrity, fabulous wealth alongside direst poverty, fame with despair. She was used to bright lights, to a city pulsing with nervous excitement, to sophisticated people and their parties. He had lived many places. One week in a human zoo like New York made him as jumpy as a caged bobcat. He craved the peace and quiet and wildness of flat, open country. He liked people that didn't know so much, that didn't care so much, that didn't talk so much.

He didn't want her glittering life any more than she would want his solitary one. They would have to part, or they would destroy each other.

Yet he knew this wanting was different. It was like a fierce thirst, and even a long drink wouldn't be enough to satisfy him. He would want her again and again.

There would be a last time to hold her, a last time to taste her lips, to take in the sweetness of her body. A last time to make love to her—the worst last time of all.

He would have to make every moment they had together count.

At the thought of that last goodbye, a bittersweet pain tore through him, intensifying until it felt as though some vital organ had been ripped out.

He pulled her closer, laid his cheek against her hair, running his hand soothingly along her neck, down the length of her back.

It no longer bothered him to hold her, to want her. Every moment with her seemed infinitely precious.

He knew that some part of him would never want to let her go.

But he was a man used to letting go, a man used to losing everything he ever loved.

The next morning Dawn was better. When she stirred, Kirk shut his eyes and pretended to be asleep so she wouldn't feel embarrassed. She got up slowly, like a goddess awakening. Shimmering sunlight sifted through the folds of the tent and splashed her slim back with golden glowing fire. She was pale, ethereal, like a creature from a lovely dream.

Through the curtain of his thick lashes he watched her pull the white cotton gown over her breasts. It fell in heavy folds past her ankles, swallowing her like a little girl putting on her mother's dress. In the shapeless white gown, with her raven hair spilling to her waist and her waiflike eyes shining shyly, she was exquisite.

But he wished she was still naked.

When she looked at him, even though he shut his eyes again, he felt his skin heating.

She came to him, lay down lazily beside him, draped a hand across his belly and waited for him to wake up.

"I'm awake," he murmured huskily.

She touched his cheek with feather-light fingers, tracing the smooth hard line of his clean-shaven jaw very tenderly. "I know," she whispered.

His mouth quirked. "How..."

"You were watching me." There was no embarrassment, no shyness in her expression. "And you were blushing."

He blushed again, and then smiled sheepishly, charmingly. "I was?"

She bent over him caressing his cheek. "I thought you didn't like skinny girls, macho man."

His eyes burned her like fire. He caught her hand, held it prisoner in his long dark fingers before sliding his palm against hers, bringing hers to his lips, and blowing a warm kiss against her wrist. "I was wrong."

She shivered.

"And I thought you didn't like macho-men Neanderthals," he taunted with an insolent grin when her pulse leapt beneath his nibbling lips.

She hesitated, and he watched the warm tide of color rise in her cheeks.

"I was wrong, too," she admitted, thinking that without his beard to mar the fine-chiseled lines of his dark face, he was stunningly handsome. "You're beautiful," she whispered with glowing eyes.

"That's supposed to be my line, princess."

"Then why did you let me beat you to it?"

"Maybe I don't like to rush a girl," he drawled in a low, soft tone.

She traced a fingertip across his belly. "And do you have—a girl, Mr. Macho cowboy... Lots of girls?" she drawled, sexily mimicking his Texas accent.

His other hand folded over the one on his stomach so that he held both her hands. His fathomless eyes were dark and seeking. "There's one—I want to have."

As his hands tensed on hers, and he started to draw her closer, her bones turned to water. Dawn was too conscious of that long bronzed body, of the intimacies they had shared and of her own nudity beneath the white gown.

They were in bed. Every night since she'd know him, she'd gone to sleep in his arms.

His handsome face was darkly flushed. The emotions he normally kept under iron control were surging to the surface.

Blood pounded in her head like a desert drumbeat. Warily she licked her dry lips. Never before had she known a man like him. Without the desert robes to conceal the power of his sun-darkened male physique, he seemed bigger, more dangerous. He exuded male virility. It didn't matter that only minutes before she'd awakened naked in his arms and found that she'd crawled on top of him once again like an uninhibited wanton, that she'd probably lain that way for hours. It didn't matter that she could still feel the burning imprint his hard warm body had left on hers.

Suddenly she felt young and very unsure, not at all the uninhibited creature of the night. She began to tremble. "K-Kirk... I-I..."

She was at a loss.

"Honey," he whispered tenderly, soothing her hair. "You don't have to be afraid... of anything. Not from me." He kept stroking her hair, and slowly her rapid and uneven breathing eased. But she avoided his eyes.

An awkward long-lasting silence enveloped them.

"W-what happened to our camel?" she blurted at last in an uncertain, childish tone. Then she blushed at the stupidity of her question, at her incredible awkwardness with him.

"The...camel?" He smiled faintly and released her hands, glad in a way that she was releasing him from the bonds of sexual tension. "I can't imagine why you'd ask about that miserable, flea-ridden beast."

Strangely, the minute Kirk let her go, she longed for him to hold her again. What was wrong with her? Why did just being near him confuse her so?

"B-because he nearly died carrying me," came her soft, mortified voice.

"He's been tended to. I thought he was finished, but it's impossible to kill anything as foul humored as that he-devil. One long drink and he tried to bite my arm off."

She relaxed.

"I can see that you understand that instinct."

"Oh, don't tease me about that! Please! I-I would never, never bite you again!"

"I might not mind...a nibble or two...under certain circumstances," he said softly, his white grin bold.

When she went red to the ears, his grin faded instantly. "Are you okay? Do you feel all right?"

"I feel like I'm starving."

"You probably are. It's way past time I got up and fixed you something to eat."

She stretched languidly. "And like I could sleep two whole days."

Because it was so tempting to lie beside her, Kirk arose abruptly. He was wearing nothing but red briefs, and he stood before her without the slightest degree of modesty. She could look or not, for all he cared.

Since he was a safe distance away, and she didn't think he was watching her, her eyes devoured him. Her shy gaze traced his large male body that was dangerously honed by smooth teak muscle, noting that there was no part of him that was not muscle, no part of him that was not dark. There were two purplish scars on his back. He'd told her that he'd been shot in Mexico and nearly died trying to rescue two kidnap victims.

As he moved, stooping down to pick up his desert robes, she noted the ripple of muscle, the beautiful raw grace of his movements.

All dancers admired beautiful bodies, male or female. Her glance traveled approvingly down his scarred back to his waist, down his legs. Kirk, who was secretly basking beneath her shining gaze, was watching her covertly.

Then her eyes froze in horror. Her mouth gaped open. She clamped it closed and looked away, hoping he hadn't seen her bitter disappointment.

But he had.

"What's the matter now?" Kirk demanded, his male vanity stung that anything about his body might displease her.

"Nothing," she murmured, but he knew she was lying when she refused to look at him.

He strode angrily over to where she was reclining.

"Tell me," he commanded.

"It's not your fault," she murmured dismally, lifting her white face to his dark one for a moment and then bowing her head once more. "The last thing I want...is to hurt your feelings...after all you've done."

"Just tell me what part of me fails to come up to your standards," came his deep, cold voice.

Her eyes were glued to his feet. "Oh, dear..."

"Tell me!"

"Oh, I can't... Oh... The most important parts!" Her tone was a dying whisper.

He sank down beside her, their despair now mutual. "No woman has ever complained before," he ground out unhappily.

"You've got flat feet!" she wailed. "How could such a beautiful man have flat feet?"

He couldn't believe what he was hearing. "Is that all?"

She was nodding forlornly. "To a dancer that's everything."

He grabbed her and crushed her to him, bursting into a rowdy rumble of relieved laughter.

"Don't you understand? I could never, never love a man who had flat feet," she whispered.

He was still laughing, his good humor fully restored. He lifted her face to his.

"Princess, there's a first time for everything."

"But good feet are the single-most important attributes a man could have."

"You have a great deal to learn about men," he murmured on a low chuckle, "and I would think it an honor if you choose me to be the one to teach you all you'll ever need to know."

Then he kissed her, slowly, softly and thoroughly, filling her with such sensual warmth and wildness, she decided languorously that maybe, just maybe, he knew what he was talking about.

Kirk stayed with Azid two days. He hadn't wanted to stay so long. He knew how quickly Aslam could track them and kill them if he decided they were worth the trouble. But Dawn needed to rest and eat and regain her strength, and

Kirk hadn't the heart to force her into the desert again so soon.

On the third day they set out, fresh from a long night's rest. This time they had two good camels, and they had only ten hours across open country before they'd reach a safe house in a mountainous village near the border.

The trip was uneventful. They passed an ancient fortress city ringed by four miles of thick ruined walls, a vast temple of the sun. The terrain changed as they climbed higher into hills covered with a brown nap, as soft as velveteen. Beneath them dark green streaks marked the canyons where there was water. As they climbed ever higher to three thousand feet, the air grew delightfully cool.

They reached a whitewashed, two-story house at dusk. Dawn couldn't believe that there was a garden behind the house with chrysanthemums, asters, hydrangeas and snapdragons. Kirk was immediately on guard, but to Dawn, after the desert, the charming house with the green mountains behind it, the quiet courtyards, the overhanging balconies, the oriel windows and closely woven screens of carved wood, all seemed a picturesque paradise. Despite her enthusiasm, Kirk was wary, studying it from afar for a long while.

Something was wrong. He felt it in his gut.

It was different from before.

At last he decided to reveal himself and bring Dawn and the camels.

An Arab and his wife rushed out to greet them. They were overly friendly and their accent was not of the desert or the mountains.

The old couple who'd lived in the house before were gone. Where? Why?

Kirk's gut twisted, but he made no outward show of his uneasiness. They had seen him. It would be certain death to try to cross the mountains at night. He yanked on the nose rope of the camel Dawn was on, pulled him to the ground and lifted her off.

As Kirk led Dawn inside, he knew they were walking into a trap.

Six

***

Kirk paced restlessly out onto the balcony and studied the jagged darkening mountains soaring thousands of feet against a violet sky. The house was enveloped in an ominous quiet.

Slitted eyes slowly, carefully scanned everything. The courtyard and gardens seemed peaceful enough.

Kirk sensed danger in every pore in his body.

It was important that he not show it—even to Dawn. They were being watched. He could feel it.

Dawn was enchanted with the house, its setting, the smell of roasting lamb and sweet tea bubbling over a samovar that drifted up from the kitchen. She felt very far and very safe from Aslam. She was thinking, tomorrow they would be truly safe. But then Kirk might put her on a plane by herself back to New York and disappear out of her life forever. Tonight might be their last night together.

The Arab couple had assumed they were married and had given them only one room. Dawn had gone into the bedroom first, and Kirk had followed her, closing the door, leaning his great body against it until she turned. Her startled eyes had gone from the double bed to his dark unreadable expression, and she had blushed as though aware for the first time of the intimacy of sharing a real bedroom with him. His own body went still and hot and tense. Abruptly he had looked away and stalked past her to the balcony.

Dawn was now filling a brass bathtub with water from steaming kettles that the Arab woman had heated over the fire and brought upstairs. Kirk came back inside from the balcony and silently watched the process for a time. The kerosene lamp made her skin glow like gold.

Her slightest movement was filled with infinite sensual grace. Suddenly he felt uncomfortable. Never before had he been forced to live so intimately with a woman. He had never wanted such closeness. Somehow this woman had opened a door to some secret place inside him, a place he'd wanted locked forever. Five days alone with her, and she was a devouring fire in the center of him; a stark, vivid longing that consumed his every thought, his every emotion.

She was a beautiful, gentle creature, an innocent girl in a hostile, barbarous land. He felt an awesome responsibility toward her. He couldn't fail her. At the thought, his face went grim. He had to keep his hands off her, his wits sharp.

When the tub was full he offered to leave so that she could bathe in privacy. He needed to go out, to check on things, to get away from her.

She glanced at him, her upturned face rosily flushed from her task, the flickering golden light lambent in her luminous eyes. He wanted her, and to conceal his feelings, he hardened his expression.

Uncertainly she caught her lower lip with her teeth. "I'd feel safer with you here," she whispered.

So she sensed it, too, he thought silently, knowing he couldn't leave her, no matter how much he wanted to. Not if she was afraid.

She began to unhook her gown, and he forgot the danger. All he could think of was the woman. As he watched those golden fingertips descend, peeling white cotton from her long, beautiful throat, a sudden tremor shook him. Dear God! What did she think he was made of—stone? Her fingers hovered at the last hook between the creamy swell of her breasts. Kirk closed his eyes and took a deep breath.

Then, as if she felt the intensity of his burning gaze, her eyes rose slowly to his again, and for a long moment they stared at one another across the room through the mist rising from the steaming tub. A sudden quick heat flamed in his body, and he shifted his weight uneasily from one foot to the other. She blushed, twisting her hands and then clasping them shyly behind her back. A muscle ticked in his cheek. Raggedly he ran a hand through his tousled hair. Then quickly he crossed the room, turned his back and threw himself into a chair so she could complete her undressing.

By accident she had left a brass pitcher on the table, and from where he sat he was riveted by her reflection. He caught his breath, clenched his hands into fists and tried not to look at her, but he couldn't stop himself.

She stepped out of her gown and let it pool at her ankles on the red-tiled floor. He sat statue still, his heart pounding violently, as he watched her scoop her long silken hair into a loose knot at the top of her head. A single strand slid through her fingers and dangled in a provocative damp coil against the curve of her neck. He wanted to go to her and lift the wayward tendril and repin it for her. He imagined her turning slowly, coming into his arms, the eagerness of her lips beneath his.

Kirk ached to rip off his clothes and assuage his raging passion.

She lifted a graceful leg delicately over the rim of the tub. Then her slender body sank languidly beneath the hot water.

He fought to remind himself of the danger around them, but he was hypnotized by her budding sensuality. He could think of nothing but the desire to take her in his arms and make her his woman.

Hungrily his eyes slid over her, lingering on her breasts. She lifted a cup and scooped water out of the tub and poured it over her shoulders, and he watched the glistening rivulets run across her golden skin and moistly heat her nipples. He watched delicious spirals of steam curl up and caress her face.

He wanted to jump out of his chair, to touch her, to caress her. He wanted it more than anything he'd ever wanted, but he knew that this time he did not dare to because he would never be satisfied with mere touching.

He closed his eyes, trying to shut out the vision that aroused such agonized need. Then he opened them again just as she lifted another cup. More dazzling rivulets followed the same hot path down her glowing skin.

Desperately he swallowed and wiped his sweating brow with the back of his hand. Then he sank lower in the chair, struggling to control his breath and racing pulse.

It was cool in the room. He felt he would burst with explosive heat. He knew he should say something, throw a towel over the pitcher—anything. She lolled back in bliss, and her hair came loose and flowed in waves to sweep the floor. Her body was relaxed, open to his view. He was rigid, every muscle paralyzed from the emotion that gripped him.

He studied the long curve of her pale golden neck. No woman he'd ever known had had such a pretty neck, throat and shoulders. Funny, but he'd never realized how erotic a lovely neck could be on a woman.

She was exquisite. Every day she seemed to grow more beautiful to him. God, why couldn't he make himself look away? It seemed despicable, watching her, pretending to have his back turned, her not knowing.

Then she took the washcloth, lifted a graceful leg and soaped it from her toes to her thighs. His blood pounded so hard and so fast, he thought he would die.

He wanted to turn around, to strip out of his own clothes and take her in his arms. He wanted to kiss her—everywhere—from her navel to thigh, until she was as hot and ready as he. He could almost taste the velvet-fluid womanly essence of her.

He had to remember where they were.

Blood ran like fire in his veins. There was a hard knot in his gut.

He thought of the long nights when he'd held her in his arms. The torture of wanting her more every night than the night before. But this was worse, even than that.

He struggled to remember the danger swirling around them.

Kirk didn't feel like talking, but he was going mad. He had to do something. He got up out of the chair almost kicking it over backward, keeping his back to her, his huge, muscled body rigid. He swore softly, viciously beneath his breath.

He lifted the pitcher and then set it back down with a clank as if the metal that had contained her image burned him.

"H-hey, D-Dawn..."

"Mmmm?" she replied drowsily, deliciously, lifting her other leg to soap it.

"So tell me about yourself, princess." His voice was strangely hoarse.

She held the washcloth poised on her glistening thigh and leaned forward. "Are you okay? You sound kind of funny," she murmured breathily.

Kirk clenched his hands and unclenched them. "Throat's a little dry...that's all...the desert." He knew he sounded like an idiot. "So, tell me how you came to be a ballerina."

She began scrubbing her breasts with the cloth. "I thought you were the guy that didn't like that kind of small talk."

"So I've changed." He bit his bottom lip. "We've been together day and night for nearly six days...and nights. I'm curious."

"It sure took a while for you to get...curious."

His eyes flicked to the fiery vision of the golden woman. "I had a few things on my mind."

"Like terrorists and dying camels and nursing me."

No! Like you! he wanted to scream. Did she know nothing of men?

"You've been wonderful, Kirk. Nobody's ever been more wonderful. When we started out I thought you..." Her voice softened. "Never mind what I thought then. It was stupid of me to have brought it up."

"No, tell me." Why did her opinion of him matter so desperately?

"I thought you were rough and crude, some sort of macho barbarian, the kind of Southern male that hasn't a trace of sensitivity or appreciation of the finer things in life. But I was so mistaken about you. You're the sweetest gentleman I've ever known."

She stood up and stepped out to dry off, and Kirk almost groaned out loud.

He clenched the edges of the table and leaned on his hands. "Honey," he managed in a voice as dry as dust, "you've got me all wrong. I'm the last thing from...a sweet gentleman."

"No. You were a stranger, and yet you've been kinder to me than my own—" She stopped herself. There was a note in her low tone that caught his heart. "What I mean is that there haven't ever been many people who really cared about me. I guess my father did..." Her choked voice trailed away.

"Your father?" Kirk thought immediately of Wayne, but who was she thinking of?

Her beautiful face twisted in bitter pain. "He died when I was ten," she whispered in a funny, faint voice. "That's odd. I haven't mentioned him in years. Usually I can't bear to talk about him to anyone. He was the only person who ever loved me. I—I... Always before I felt too lonely to think of him, but now...with you...somehow...I can."

"Go on," Kirk said softly.

"You don't want to hear my problems."

"Yes, I do."

She hesitated. She seemed to be fighting some inner battle with herself, just as he was doing. It was as if she didn't think Kirk could possibly want to hear her problems, but at the same time she could no longer control the deluge that came tumbling out.

"You see," she whispered on a raw sob. "M-my mother never cared about me at all. I don't know why she ever had a child in the first place. Sometimes it was hard to believe she was even my mother. I used to pray sometimes that she wasn't, that God would give me a new mother. When I was eleven I received a fully paid ballet scholarship to New York. We lived in Mexico City. The happiest moment of her life was when she put me on that plane for New York. I really haven't seen her but a couple of times since. She never writes. My own mother...just doesn't care. I really don't like to talk about her. I don't know why I did. I never do. I was eleven, in New York, in a huge ballet school. I was so alone. So scared. I didn't know what to do, where to turn. Somehow I learned to survive."

So she was not so different from him after all. Maybe that's what drew him to her, despite the intensity of his stubborn will to remain unaffected.

He wanted to go to her, to kiss away the loneliness, the bitter pain, to lose part of his own in the joy of taking her, but he dared not touch her.

Every muscle in his body tensed as she pulled her white gown over her naked body. She picked up a brush and ran it slowly, sensuously through the long waves of her hair. He watched her, hypnotized, thinking her beautiful as she brushed her hair in the golden lamplight.

"I really wasn't ever a perfect dancer, but I worked so hard, harder than anybody ever worked. Days. Nights. I had nothing else, you see, until Lincoln noticed me."

"Lincoln?"

She set the brush down. Her hair gleamed like black satin against her white gown. Kirk wanted to run his hands through it, to watch it spill through his fingers, to lift it to his face and smother his lips with the sweet silken mass.

"Lincoln Wilde. He was a prodigy and the most brilliant choreographer in the world. He's only thirty-four, but he's now the head of the New National Theater where we both work. He began to create small parts for me. I worked terribly hard. There were bigger parts. He believed in me. He was the only person who ever did."

There was something in her voice, a reverent note, that bothered Kirk, much more than he wanted it to. "And...are you in love…with this Lincoln?" he demanded in a hoarse whisper.

"Oh, he's incredibly attractive."

Kirk felt a raw knot of jealousy tear his gut.

"I suppose like every other girl in the corps, I had a crush on him for a while, even though he's impossibly arrogant. He's so big and blond and gorgeous—completely masculine, I assure you."

Not in the least pleased at this reassurance, Kirk picked up his *kaffiyeh* and wadded it into a tangled mass of cloth before thrusting it back onto the table.

"But he's married and deeply in love with someone else. She isn't even a dancer. Once I let him know how I felt, he shut me out of his personal life just as he shut her out of his professional life. I was his dancer. The instrument for his creations. Nothing more. She was his wife."

"But you wanted to be more?"

"Sometimes." Her voice was shaky. "Y-yes, I wanted more, maybe because I knew he was so safe. You see, I was afraid of love, afraid of real life, afraid of being really close to someone…because I was afraid to love and lose again. My life consisted of dreams, ballet, the stage."

Kirk had never lived on dreams; his life had been filled with harsh realities. But he knew too well what it was to be afraid of loss.

"O-oh, I don't know why I'm telling you all this," she murmured.

"Because I asked," he said softly.

Deliciously steamy and flushed from her bath, she tiptoed on bare feet across the room and touched the back of his neck with warm, delicate fingers. It was as though she felt closer to him because at last he had evinced interest in her as a person, because something in his voice had told her he understood.

At her slight touch, he whirled. They were face to face, body to body. His immense maleness dwarfed her. A breathless hush fell between them.

She was only inches from him and a thousand times more beautiful in the flesh than in the reflection. He felt mesmerized, on fire. Her eyes were shining with some soft irresistible emotion. Her soul touched his, and he knew that what he felt went much deeper than desire.

He wanted to take her into his arms, to crush her into his body, but he knew if he did, he would be lost—forever.

He had been wrong when he thought he could take her once and leave her. Wrong. He hadn't understood a damned thing about this woman, about the power of his own feelings toward her. He could never never let himself have her. Not even once. Or he would not be able to bear losing her.

"K-Kirk . . ." she whispered raggedly. Something desperate was in her eyes, too. "It's your turn to bathe. I'll sit here . . ."

Her warm breath stirred against the pulsing heartbeat at the base of his throat. He caught her delicate scent. He could almost taste her, she was so sweet, so clean. He felt her quivering innocent emotion.

There was a wildness in her. Untouched. A wildness that she did not understand, but he did.

"No!" He sent the chair flying against the wall and strode across the room a safe distance away from her. "Damn, you! No!" He was trembling violently. He felt tormented, driven to the brink by the beauty of her, by the softness. "I'm going out. I have to be alone."

He fumbled in his satchel for a gun, jammed a clip in it and removed the safety. He set it on the table. "All you have to do is pull the trigger."

Then he opened the door and walked out, banging the door shut with an inarticulate cry of rage.

She heard the thunder of his steps crashing down the stairs.

Then there was silence.

Dawn sank down upon the bed, all joy gone from her ashen face, a bitter despair closing around her heart. What had she done wrong? What had she said to him that had made him storm out in such a fury? Why must she always make mistakes with him?

She had so little time to understand him, and she had tried so hard after that first night when he had saved her, when she had behaved like such a wanton and he had rejected her so coldly. He did not want to be chased, and she had tried to contain her feelings. But it was so hard.

For him, to win his respect, she'd endured the desert in silence, even when she'd believed she was dying. She'd ridden the camel for him, she who'd never once even gotten on a horse. Then at Azid's camp, Kirk had nursed her so tenderly, and afterward he'd seemed friendlier, more open to her.

Now it was as if he hated her all over again.

Any time she ever got close to him, he deliberately recoiled, shutting her out.

At last she turned out the lamp and lay down in the dark, feeling frightened, but leaving the lamp out because she was afraid he would never come until he thought she was asleep. A long time later her heart constricted when she heard the sound of his footsteps as he wearily climbed the stairs. It hurt so much that he wanted nothing to do with her.

The door opened and closed. She was aware of him standing in the dark, of his eyes studying the way she sheets molded the lines of her body. Her body felt on fire beneath his gaze. Then he began to undress. The sound of his clothes falling to the floor sent a strange tremor through her.

The mattress dipped with the weight of his body. Though he did not touch her, she felt the heat of him seeping beneath the covers, and she was comforted.

She wished he wasn't so set against her. She wished she could turn to him and cuddle up in his arms. Instead she lay in rigid, lonely silence. It was odd that he seemed not to be so threatened by her need for closeness when she was asleep and would accept her then.

When Dawn awoke later in the dead of the night and reached for Kirk, he was gone.

She knew instantly that something was dreadfully wrong.

Outside she heard some sound, footsteps on stone.

The night seemed a living thing, pressing down upon her. She wanted to hide beneath the covers, to cower in the relative safety of her bed.

But where was Kirk? What if he was in danger?

Slowly she crept out of bed, careful to keep her footsteps soundless. Quickly she stripped out of her cumbersome gown and put on her ragged tights and torn costume. Then she crawled out onto the balcony.

In the moonlight she could make out shadowy figures running in the courtyard.

They had Kirk. Two men were holding him, and another was beating him senseless.

There was a stake in the middle of the courtyard, ropes, guns. They were enjoying themselves before they tied him to the stake and shot him.

They they would come after her.

A man in black was standing apart. The moon came out, and a shaft of brilliance glinted across his dark features. She would have known that cruel face with the curved dagger's nose anywhere. A shiver of terror traced the length of her spine.

Aslam!

There were sounds in the rooms below, and she knew that they were coming for her.

Quickly she crawled back inside the bedroom, bolted the door, and then picked up the gun from the table. She raced outside onto the balcony again, looking down, wondering if she should scream or jump.

There was no way she could get to Kirk except by running along the roofs, jumping from roof to roof until she could reach the courtyard. The buildings were not so far apart, and yet no one but a dancer would have considered such a thing. She limped to the farthest edge of the balcony, hesitated for a long moment as she judged the leap necessary to grab the tile edge hanging over the eave. For an instant she touched the medallion at her throat. Then she willed the pain from her ankle and ran, leaping at just the last moment, arching, flying. Her nails dug into tiles and stone. Her body dangled thirty feet above flagstones.

A roof tile came loose and fell with a clatter. She had no idea if the men below heard, if even now they were aiming their rifles at her struggling swinging form that was perfectly silhouetted against the white wall.

It took all her strength, but she managed to stretch and cling, grabbing handhold after handhold, until at last she hauled her lithe body onto the roof.

She looked down. The men were still beating Kirk. They were going to kill him if she didn't stop them. Suddenly, as those other times before, she knew that all this had happened to her before in some long-ago forgotten time. This was some ancient nightmare come to life.

The figures swirled like dancing devils in a white hot flame.

No....

The flame was inside her, possessing her, obliterating every rational thought.

The figures were dragging Kirk's limp body to the stake. Others were shouldering their guns expectantly.

Dawn had a flash of dread. This was her last chance! In another minute he would be dead.

She had to keep panic at bay, or it would be too late to save Kirk.

The flame rose higher, and she sank to the roof in despair, devoured in the radiant bosom of its fire. Frantically she touched the medallion at her throat.

The last thing she heard was a sound, like a demonic cry, louder than anything she had ever heard before, piercing the silence. She had no idea what it was. Vaguely, she was aware of a shattering pain in her ankle.

The moon slid behind a mountain, but she had no realization that it did so.

They were going to kill Kirk! And then come after her! And she couldn't stop them because she was being swallowed alive in some blazing flame from hell.

Something snapped. Her world went black.

When she came to, she was in the courtyard, her breath coming in harsh rasps, as if she'd exerted herself physically to the extreme limits of her ability. Even after dancing the most difficult ballets, she'd never felt this drained. She had the fiercest headache of her life, and her ankle was throbbing with an intense and inexplicable pain.

The three men who had been beating Kirk lay unconscious on the ground. Aslam was cowering on the flagstones, his body a quivering mass, and a breathless battlecrazed Kirk had a gun shoved into the Arab's belly. "Call off your men, or you die."

"One man against so many?" Aslam tried to laugh. His eyes glimmered with fanatical hate, but with fear, also. "They will kill you . . . and then the girl."

Kirk kicked him savagely. "But you will die first."

There was a long silence, and then Kirk's hand moved on the trigger.

At the last second Aslam screamed something in Arabic.

"Tell them to put down their guns," Kirk commanded.

More hysterical Arabic.

"Tell them to open the cellar door and get inside it," Kirk continued.

"If you shut us in there, we might never get out."

"That's your problem."

As if in a dream, Dawn listened to Aslam giving orders to his men; she watched his men filing one by one down the cellar stairs. The last to go was the Arabian couple who had betrayed them. Then Kirk yanked Aslam to his feet and shoved him screaming down the stairs.

Kirk locked the doors behind them. He spent a long time securing the doors, laying stones and heavy pieces of equipment on the doors.

Despite the cold air, he was sweating from the exertion when he finished. He turned toward her, his face alight with passionate admiration. Never in her wildest fantasy had she dreamed that he could ever look at her with such an expression.

She flung herself into his arms.

"Oh, Kirk," she sobbed into his chest. "You're all right. I thought . . . I was so afraid . . ."

He held her tightly. His hard fingers ruffled her hair ever so gently. Then he held her away from him and studied her, his eyes glowing with awe.

"You saved my life," she whispered brokenly.

"Honey," he murmured. "It was the other way around."

Her eyes widened. "What?"

"I've never seen anything like it. They were tying me up, about to shoot me. You came off that roof with your eyes as wild as an insane she-cat, scratching, clawing, shooting, screaming. I strangled the guy tying me up, got his gun, got to Aslam. You're a natural soldier, the kind that comes to life in the thick of things. I never knew a woman..." His voice softened. "You're one hell of a woman."

She listened to him in amazement. All she remembered was the vivid blaze of white filling her with a wild terror.

"I—I thought I fainted... I don't remember any of it."

"Things happened so fast, none of them knew what to do. You were incredible, wonderful."

She stared at him blankly. "Nothing."

"You mean, you really don't remember?"

She shook her head. She thought of those other white flashes and wondered briefly what they meant. "S-sometimes I think... I forget things."

"You saved my life," he whispered. "I don't know how I'll ever repay you."

She let her head fall limply against his chest. She felt the warm, steady beating of his heart. "I have what I wanted. You're still alive," she murmured. "I—I'm not sure I can walk. I think I hurt my ankle."

"It doesn't matter. After what you did I'll gladly carry you every step of the way."

He lifted her into his arms, and she felt very tiny and very feminine sheltered closely against his powerful body as he moved toward the house.

"I don't know about you, but for me the hydrangeas and snapdragons have lost their charm. What do you say we get the hell out of here?"

"In the dark?" She turned her face to him. He kissed her mouth softly.

"Real soldiers aren't afraid of the dark," he murmured.

"So... I'm not a real soldier."

"It doesn't matter. The sun will be up in an hour. Until then, I'll fend off the monsters of the night. It's my turn to take care of you."

Seven

A sigh of fear escaped Dawn's throat as she clutched Kirk's sleeve. Three days had passed since the cottage in the mountains. They had trekked across two countries in a jeep, in a broken-down truck, on foot.

They were in the Istanbul airport, and he was going to put her on a plane. He was leaving her, sending her back to her own world as she'd known he would, and there seemed nothing she could do to dissuade him.

The airport swarmed as busily as an anthill. Dark-skinned people in flowing robes with long sleeves and bright fabrics shoved and shouted in the long lines behind the ticket counters, their passionate voices mingling into cacophonous thunder. On an open grill, a man was cooking eggplant, shish kebab and goat meat. Strangely, nowhere else had Dawn felt more terribly alone or more abandoned than in this bustling madhouse.

"Passports, please," the man behind the ticket counter insisted when Kirk pushed his way to the front of the line.

"The lady's lost hers," Kirk said grimly.

"Then we can't book her to London."

Dawn stood behind Kirk, holding onto his arm. Kirk had bought her a pair of jeans and a purple silk blouse. Her ankle was wrapped in an Ace bandage. He was wearing black slacks and a black shirt. They clung to his massive muscled body like a second skin. She didn't want him to send her away, but she could think of no way to stop him.

The mission was over as far as he was concerned, and so was his involvement with her. He'd made that very clear the night before when he'd walked her up to her hotel room after they'd had dinner. When they'd reached her door, he had towered beside her, vitally masculine. He'd stood so close to her that she'd had to tilt her head back to see his face. Only an inch or two had separated their bodies, and though she'd longed for him to take her into his arms, he had not touched her. An impenetrable mask had covered his dark features, but the searing passion in his eyes had jolted through her.

"Why did you save me?" she asked softly as she handed him her room key.

Her fingers touched his briefly, yet so tantalizingly, that he'd jumped at even this slight contact with her. Her own pulse quickened. His dark eyes had slanted from the brass key in his open palm to her upturned face, lingering on her mouth, then back to the key before he'd jammed it into the lock.

"You'll find out," he muttered hastily.

When the door didn't open and she moved closer, he swore quietly, as though all his frustrations were centered on the lock.

"But not now?" she queried softly.

"No."

"And not from you?"

"That's right," he muttered harshly. His hands were shaking as he worked with the perverse lock and key. He was not immune to her.

She came even closer, until she was almost touching him, and whispered, "I think . . . maybe . . . you're turning it the wrong way."

He twisted the key in the opposite direction and the lock clicked.

"There!" she exclaimed triumphantly.

His eyes met hers and she felt the passion in him, blazing just below the surface. She took a shallow breath.

"You want me, too . . ." she whispered.

He shook his head and backed away, clenching his fists as he retreated deeper into the shadows.

"Yes, you do! But you're just going to walk out on me."

"I'm putting you on a plane to London in the morning. You'll be okay." He turned to go to his own room.

"No!" she cried across the darkness, knowing that the last thing she should do was chase him.

"Look . . ." Something unreadable came and went in his eyes. "It's better this way."

"Stay with me," she pleaded. "Just for tonight."

She felt his eyes move over her body. His gaze was hot and brilliant, his dark face flushed. Everywhere his eyes touched her, her skin burned. A muscle ticked savagely along his jawline. His entire body shuddered, but he clenched his teeth together. "No."

"Not even when you know I'm scared of the dark?"

"Leave the lights on then, princess," he ordered, "and lock your door." Then he vanished into the darkness, and she'd spent the night alone with only her wadded pillow to hug as she dreamed of him coming to her and folding her into his arms.

A Gypsy woman, racing for a plane, bumped into Dawn, and she held onto Kirk more tightly. Why, oh, why was he so anxious to be rid of her?

Kirk turned back from the ticket counter, his handsome face dark with fury. "Damn. I never met a Turk before that wouldn't take a bribe."

Dawn was filled with a wild joy. Kirk couldn't put her on the plane. He wasn't going to leave her...yet.

He grabbed her by the hand and pulled her through the milling, jostling throng.

"Where are we going?" she cried.

For a long moment he made no answer. "I can't leave you in Turkey. Aslam has men here, connections."

She paled.

Kirk's eyes were steady as they met hers. "Honey, don't worry," he said in a gentle, soothing tone. "I'll get you out...no matter what I have to do."

She fought to appear brave to him but could manage only a quavery smile.

He thought she looked young and very vulnerable. He remembered how beautiful she'd been last night when she'd offered herself to him, how much he'd wanted her, how it had torn him apart to leave her. He couldn't fail her and let Aslam get her again. Nor did Kirk intend to wait days for a passport.

Kirk's hand tightened convulsively around her fingers and he pulled her through the crowd, outside into the blazing heat of the brilliant morning. For a long moment he just stood there, his great body tense, his mind a furious whirl as he scanned the airport and tried to think what to do.

"Damn!"

There was the smell of jet fuel, the scurry of baggage cars, the roar of jet engines. Kirk dragged her across what seemed like miles of concrete and asphalt until at last they reached a battered hangar. They went inside to a shabby office with an ancient, slowly-rotating overhead fan. A fat Turk with bulging black eyes and a dirty white suit was holding court behind a scarred desk.

"I want to rent an airplane." Kirk held out a thick wad of hundred-dollar bills. "A jet. The best you've got."

For a moment there was no sound other than the faint whine of the fan. Then the Turk waved his hand in dismissal, and his friends got up and went out to the hangar, one by one. He pulled out a knife and began to clean a black fingernail. "You need to be a Turkish citizen."

"Hell."

But the man seemed hypnotized by the wad of money. He set his knife on his desk. "Of course, we could provide you with a pilot. There would be no problem as long as you do not go outside of Turkey. Then we would need passports, certain documents, a few formalities..."

"I'm a pilot, damn it."

The Turk cast one last regretful look at the money, picked up his knife and carved out the filth beneath a second nail. "Then, I'm sorry, sir."

The private jet was cleared for takeoff. Kirk roared down the runway. Dawn clutched her armrest and watched concrete rush by in a sickening blur as the plane lifted into a vast cobalt sky. Behind the cockpit doors, in the cabin, Dawn tried not to hear the struggles of the pilot who was bound hand and foot to a seat.

"Where are we going?" she whispered as the jet shot higher and higher into the sky. Istanbul slid sideways. Her stomach flipped queasily, and a sudden tightness in her throat made it difficult to breathe. Kirk flew like a fighter pilot.

"I was hired to get you to London."

"But the pilot . . . in the cabin . . ."

"I didn't hurt him, and unless he does something crazy, I'm not going to."

"The plane . . . We aren't supposed . . ."

"For the money that crook charged me, I should fly you all the way to New York. After we land, the pilot can fly it back to Istanbul."

"You're breaking all kinds of international laws."

"I had to get you out."

"W-where did you learn to fly like this?"

"My sister's a pilot. She got me interested."

They were over the Mediterranean. Streaking over dazzling blue, over tiny ships, craggy islands. Then the jet shot straight up into the sky.

Dawn felt a rush of exhilaration as she covertly glanced at Kirk at the controls. He was wild. Wild. And his wildness was filling her. The world seemed very far beneath them. It was as if their separate lives, their separate worlds, were down there too, lost, unimportant to both of them. There was only this moment. Only Kirk. She felt alive in every cell in her body.

She began to laugh, and he turned to her, faintly alarmed. "What's wrong?"

"You're wild," she whispered. Her beautiful face was aglow. Her eyes were brilliant. "I've never known anyone like you before. I've never felt like this. So out of control. It's fun to feel like anything in the whole world is possible! Absolutely anything!" *Even us,* she thought, and then let the thought die away.

Her head was thrown back, her lovely long throat exposed, her laughter a soft velvet sound that seemed to reach even the most secret places in his heart.

He smiled at her, his rugged face gentle, and the effect was devastating.

Her laughter died in her throat. Slowly her eyes met his. *Even us,* she longed to whisper.

A breathless hush fell between them. He had not touched her since they'd gotten safely into Turkey.

He lifted her hand and kissed her wrist, and she shivered when she felt his hot mouth against her naked skin.

A fever pulsed from his warm lips directly into her bloodstream.

The jet was safely on the ground, taxiing the length of the runway at Heathrow Airport. A swarm of police cars with screaming sirens was careening toward the jet as Kirk brought it to a stop.

A voice from a loudspeaker was issuing a battery of commands and threats to the outlaws in the Turkish jet. Kirk was about to open the door, when Dawn touched his sleeve. She looked up at him, her face shining, yet frightened.

"I—I'll never be able to thank you," she whispered, her voice choked with feeling.

"It's enough that you're safe." His low tone was husky, and his eyes were disarmingly gentle. He crooked his finger and touched her cheek, and then jerked his hand away.

Dawn stared up at him wordlessly. "I'm sorry you're in so much trouble because of me."

"I've been in trouble all my life," he said. "If there's anything I know how to handle, it's trouble."

She was thinking that he'd risked his life, everything for her. She drew a breath. There was no telling what the men outside might do to him. This tall, strangely silent stranger had shown her more kindness than anyone in her whole life ever had before.

In a burst of emotion she flung her arms around his neck and kissed him. A ripple of excitement coursed through them both.

He had vowed never to touch her again, but nothing on earth had ever felt so good as the small slim body pressed into his, as the sweet flutter of hot lips opening beneath his.

He was caught in a swirling mist of passion, and he could not stop himself from arching her body into his. Beneath flimsy purple silk his fingers slid over the rounded shape of her breasts, and he held her tightly against his hardening body for the longest charged moment in either of their lives. He drew in a fierce sharp breath. His eyes closed and he bent over her, his kisses harder this time, hotter.

His arms drew her up against him until she was so tightly pressed against him it seemed as though the heat of his body must fuse her to him. His mouth moved against hers, his tongue moist and urgent as it slid between her still-parted lips. As he tasted her, she sighed. Instinctively her hands crept around his neck and clung.

He bent her backward, this wanting fiercer than anything he'd ever experienced. Always before he'd looked upon women as necessary to his pleasure when they were available. Something he could live without when they were not. Flames of passion engulfed him. Body and soul, he felt fused to her.

This woman was different. Utterly, completely different.

He felt her shudder. His body began to tremble. Abruptly he let her go. For a moment he couldn't tear his blazing eyes from her beautiful, desire-flushed face. There were tears in her eyes. Her sorrowful expression ripped his soul to pieces. He started to say something, and then realized there was nothing to say except goodbye, and somehow he lacked the strength to say it.

He had to put her out of his mind, out of his heart.

He turned and opened the door.

Twelve men rushed up the stairs and tore his hand from hers.

She watched them manhandle him down the stairs and then slam him roughly against a waiting car with flashing lights and search him.

Then an officer yanked Kirk's hands behind his back and brutally handcuffed him.

"No!" she screamed, stricken by this final humiliation. "No! You don't understand!"

She knew Kirk heard her voice because he flinched. But he kept his black head bowed and would not look at her. They shoved him inside the car.

When she raced down the stairs and tried to reach him, she was surrounded by reporters.

They considered her a world-famous ballerina, to be feted and pampered.

They considered him nothing more than a common criminal.

Moonlight glinted off the Thames. The long, eighteenth-century windows of the mirrored studio attached to her friend's charming flat were open, and gauzy curtains curled in the soft, damp breeze.

Dawn lay on a couch in a corner, feeling wretchedly miserable and lost, sipping a glass of wine even though the wine merely intensified her feelings of loneliness. After the police had let her go and she'd escaped the siege of reporters clamoring for her story, she'd taken a taxi to an English ballerina's flat in Chelsea, only to find her friend, Sheri, gone. Dawn had located the key under a pot in the garden and had let herself inside.

She refilled her glass. There was a gnawing ache in her stomach and a constant pain in her chest where her heart was. She had tried to do some stretches and warm-up exercises, but all she could think of was Kirk. All evening she'd kept flicking on the television and listening to the story concerning her escape. At least the press was making him into an international hero. Why couldn't the police see that he wasn't a hijacker, that he'd had to do what he'd done.

They had to let him go. They had to. She'd done everything she could to make them see that. Lincoln had appealed to everyone of any importance that he knew in London. Finally the police had allowed Kirk to make a couple of phone calls. Within an hour there had been a call from Washington. Things had seemed to calm down after that.

The doorbell rang at midnight, buzzing over and over again before she heard it above the music.

When she stumbled across the forecourt and elaborate gateway to the double doors, the last person she expected to see on the twisting staircase was a brooding, darkly-tanned Kirk with his heavy satchel slung over his shoulder. His silver bracelet gleamed in the moonlight. He stood on the bottom step, as if he'd been on the verge of leaving.

They each were very still, regarding one another silently, a raw elemental tension leaping between them.

"They let you go... with the money?" she whispered.

"Friends in high places," he murmured in a deep, raspy voice. "You helped too, you know, fighting for me so hard. If you hadn't made them let me make those calls..."

His chiseled features were harsh yet handsome. That wayward black lock tumbled across his brow. His eyes were so deep and dark and intense that she shivered.

In the background she could hear the music filtering from the studio as it rose to a crescendo. A wild, thrilling excitement filled her, drumming along her nerve ends. It was a struggle to keep her voice calm.

"I thought you'd just go back to wherever you came from when they let you out."

The music enveloped them.

"I was going to. The authorities want me out of England—fast. I was boarding a chartered plane for the States, but all I could think of was you—jumping down from that roof, fighting like a wildcat to save me. I kept thinking about the way you pleaded my case with the police, the way you made me out to be such a hero to the press, the way you told me where to reach you when I was released. I kept seeing your face, your eyes. I kept remembering how you felt in my arms. I've never known anybody like you before. No woman... Not ever... I couldn't just walk out of your life without even saying goodbye."

She wanted so much more than goodbye.

He took her hand in his and brought it slowly to his lips. She nearly fainted when she felt his tongue, wet against her warm naked skin. When he felt her tremble he looked up, and the wanton invitation in her brilliant dark eyes dazzled him. He fought an inner battle, striving for control.

She was an innocent, but she wanted to be a woman. His woman.

"I should have gotten on that damned plane," he muttered fiercely, but the hunger in his eyes grew more intense than ever.

"No..."

He let her hand fall from his lips and leaned into her body, crushing her to him. They held onto each other as if they would die if they didn't. After a long time he let her lead him into the studio.

The mirrored room was filled with moonlight and sensuous music. In the mirrors she could see the reflection of a slim girl in a flowing skirt and a tall, powerful man.

"So you've been dancing...alone?" he whispered huskily.

"And drinking wine," she admitted.

"There are some things one should never do alone."

His voice was deep and melodious, and it blended with the music and flowed inside her. She felt a passionate fire in every part of her. The drumbeat of the music seemed to pulse at the exact tempo of her heart.

"You're thirsty then?"

"That and much more." His tone was low and charged.

She poured him a glass of wine, but he set it down beside hers.

"Dance with me," she whispered.

His eyes met hers, and he studied her for a long time, as though caught in the spell of her beauty. She was lovely with the moonlight shimmering in her hair, with the silvery light falling gently across her filmy skirts. He could think of nothing but the nearness of her soft young body.

He knew how wrong it was to have come.

He remembered her laughter in the plane, the exquisite bolt of wild joy he had felt then.

It was the same now.

He was out of control.

He had never felt better in his life.

He reached for her, spanning her tiny waist with his large hands, shaping her body against his. He felt his every muscle touch hers. For a long time they were still, savoring the delicious hot feeling of coming together.

They stood in the darkness with the moonlight sifting through billowing curtains. Tentatively her hand moved up his chest and gently circled his neck. Her nipples hardened against his chest, and his body turned to fire. It was as if she were his first, as if he'd never touched another woman before.

He began to move slowly, languidly to the music, pressing her body into his, leading her in the most sensual dancing she'd ever done.

She was barely conscious of his arms tightening around her, so caught up was she in the unbelievable sensations of his body touching hers. She felt his hips move against her own, and a fever ran in her blood. He was shaking against her, and to her surprise, Dawn realized that she was shaking, too. Suddenly she was dizzy, and her hands slid automatically over the muscles of his chest to his shoulders. Beneath his shirt she felt the pattern of smooth dark skin stretching over muscle and bone. The latent power of his body against hers sent a thrilling ripple through her.

They were in an erotic dream of their own making, dancing beneath a spotlight of moonlight, a dazzling couple floating at the center of a shaft of silvery white fire.

For most of her life she had danced.

But never like this.

Never had she danced as though she were one with the music, one with the man, and for the first time the dance was real.

She had stepped out of her dreams into a reality more dazzling than any dream.

The bedroom was wrapped in total darkness...and he was darkness, too. And for the first time in her life, she was unafraid, because he was with her, because she was discovering that there was a beauty in darkness that could never be found anywhere else, a beauty in touching, a beauty in listening to the hushed wordless sound of love, a beauty in the closeness of two bodies coming together.

He was touching her, holding her, undressing her, sliding cool silk across her heated skin, pulling her down, down beneath cold, crisp sheets and clasping her close to his searing length until every cell in her body was ablaze.

Never had she been handled with such exquisite tenderness as she was by this hard, yet gentle man.

"Kirk," she whispered. "I—I don't know how."

His fingers slid across her skin, barely touching her, yet arousing her until she was breathless.

"I—I'm so afraid . . . I'll disappoint you," she confessed.

She could smell the pleasant musky-male odor of his body, almost taste him.

Softly he entwined his fingers in her hair. His lips caressed her throat, that long beautiful throat, letting the sensuality that existed between them say what was so difficult to put into words. "Honey . . . honey . . ." he whispered. "You were born knowing. You were made for this. Just let yourself go. You're incredibly beautiful. Incredibly sweet. Incredibly brave. I don't know how I'll ever get enough of you."

"You've had all those other women."

She felt him tense. Quietly he moved his hands along her body, down her belly, touching her intimately, everywhere, stopping nowhere, using the bold sweetness of his touch to bring her close to him emotionally as well as physically. "None of them matter. There's no one but you. No one but us. No time except tonight." He leaned down and kissed her tenderly on the mouth. "There's never been anyone but you."

"Still, it'll never work, will it?"

"What?" he whispered, lifting his mouth from her throat, though he knew what she meant.

"Us." Her single word was both eloquent and sad.

He ran a finger lightly under her breast and said nothing. Then his mouth took hers again passionately. A fever that was both exquisite pleasure and exquisite pain pulsed in her blood. She had never known there could be such sorrow coupled to joy, that extreme sadness could intensify delight and make it even more precious.

He was hers tonight. She could never have him again.

After a lifetime without love, she had found it.

Only to know it couldn't last. There was only now. Only tonight and this precious hot pulsating moment.

He was the wrong man.

She was the wrong woman.

But neither of them would ever want another.

Very slowly he slanted his mouth against hers. His kiss deepened. The tip of his tongue touched hers, and they were caught in the spiral of a flame that consumed them. They were drowning in waves of velvet darkness, exchanging their separate solitudes for a completeness they could find only in each other.

In the moonlight his face was wild and dark. She did not know that her own eyes blazed just as brilliantly as his. She only knew that the passion that burned in him, burned in her as well.

His hands moved on her body, handling her with a rough yet tender expertise that left her trembling. He stroked her long neck, then buried his lips against the quickening heartbeat in the hollow of her throat. His hands slid to her breasts, caressing them until each quivering nipple throbbed beneath his touch. Then he kissed his way down her stomach, nibbling with his lips, tickling her skin with his tongue.

Kirk paid no attention to her sudden electric stillness. He kissed the inside of her navel before pressing his face lower, into her lap.

She was shaking all over, speechless with astonishment even as she entwined her fingers in his hair, clutching him closer.

The inhibitions of a lifetime were forgotten. She drew him nearer, surrendering herself completely to the fierce melting urgency his mouth stirred at the quick of her. In the rapture of his seeking lips she discovered herself, her womanliness, her utter wildness, her craven need of him.

What, oh what if she had never found him? How had she endured the terrible loneliness before him?

A soft keening like that of a creature being newly born escaped her lips.

Then the world was a rainbow of flame, and she was burning, drowning, dying. Being reborn in splintering passionate delight.

He waited for the aftershocks of her passion to subside before he drew her once more into his arms. Then he aligned her body to his, and suddenly he was inside her. There was only the tiniest flash of pain.

At her muted cry, he stopped, holding himself still so that she could grow accustomed to him. His mouth fastened slowly on hers, and she let her lips open to him endlessly. She reveled in the male sprawl of his hot body on top of hers. Lovingly she touched his hair, brushed his fevered brow.

He began to move again, gently at first, and then, when he could control himself no longer, he thrust deeply. Love that had been denied to her for years burst gloriously inside her, and she moaned against his lips. At this faint sigh of ecstasy from her, he lost what little remnant of control he still had. She felt his body tighten. His arms were like iron, binding her to him. His skin was fire. Then he was shuddering and clinging, and so was she.

After it was over, they lay breathlessly together, he cradling her close against his powerful body. She could feel the rivulets of sweat in his hair. They coursed along the side of his cheek. His breath came in harsh, urgent rasps.

She coiled herself tightly to him and listened to the violent pounding of his heart. He was everything she could have dreamed of in a lover. Everything. He had awakened a passion that had exploded through her entire being and left her feeling weak and spent and vulnerable. She could not help wondering what it had been like for him, but she lacked the courage to ask him.

She lay in his arms, silent, almost content.

The last thing she heard was his husky voice whispering a woman's name against the warm base of her throat where her pulse beat throbbed against his mouth.

"Julia... Darling Julia..."

The name was disturbing. She drifted into sleep with his hands stroking her hair.

The name haunted her even in her dreams.

She was a child again and lost. Someone was calling to her, and yet the name they used was Julia. She could not answer them, no matter how she wanted to. So she remained lost and afraid, in hiding.

She awakened and lay still in the darkness. Then she fell asleep once more.

Eight

——

Dawn dreamed, and in her dream she was dancing through swirling mists in a diamond-sprinkled darkness, dancing toward a single shaft of light coming from above. The closer she came to the light, the more brilliant it became, until finally it whitened everything. The light was like the white flame that terrified her, and yet some part of her knew she had to find out what lay beyond it. She had to stand in its light and heat. She had to feel its warmth flooding even to her bones, to her soul.

At the center of the flame was a man. He held out his arms, and she soared into them.

"Darling..."

Had he spoken or had she?

She came awake slowly, to the melodious velvet sound of the most beautiful male drawl she had ever heard.

She felt the incredible heat of his naked body as he wrapped her closer. His hands sifted through her hair.

"Bad dream?" he murmured gently.

"No. The most wonderful dream of my life. I know this sounds crazy, but I feel that at last, I've come home. I was lost, and now I'm found."

The sheets rustled, and he pulled her on top of him. "Maybe you just needed to get loved," he murmured dryly, with a smile.

"How can you insult me at a time like this when I was pouring my heart out to you?"

"It wasn't an insult," he said with a tender smile, tracing the length of her spine with his fingertip. "You're a warm-blooded, healthy young woman. You need a man."

"Not just any man," she purred. "You."

She reveled in the hot male sprawl of his body, in the masculine arms cradling her so protectively.

She touched his jawline, brushed her fingers through his hair. "Kirk, tell me who I am. Why you came after me. I have to know."

She felt his hand pause at the base of her spine.

"Honey, I told you. It's complicated. I don't think I should be the one..."

Her fingers fumbled with the medallion at her throat. "I have to know. I keep remembering things. Things I can't remember. These flashes started coming to me when Aslam kidnapped me. It was like the kidnapping triggered something—unlocked some door. Oh, I know it sounds crazy, but I remember you. Your eyes. A horse. And terror. Then there's always this white light that scares me and the headaches afterward. It's like some part of me doesn't want to remember. Like I've been running all my life from some frightening memory locked inside me. Only now, with you, I feel brave enough to face it all. I danced, you see, all the time. Because if you really dance, I mean hours and hours every day, and really concentrate, there's never any time to think, or live. I never wanted any time for those things. All of a sudden, though, I want to know what's happening to me. I have to know who I am."

"Honey..." He swallowed at the terrible emotion welling up inside him. He felt like his heart was bursting apart from the inside out. How could he tell her that all the pain and terror of these things were his fault? That her loveless childhood was his fault as well?

"You sure know how to catch a guy in a weak moment," he muttered.

"Tell me...please..."

Dawn felt his body tense, and at first she thought he would refuse her again. Then his voice filled the fluid darkness.

"Your real name is Julia Jackson."

"Julia..." He had called her that last night.

"You were kidnapped when you were a little girl. It was my fault. I was teaching you to ride. I—I...tried to save you, but I couldn't. I—I—"

His voice broke, and he was silent for a long time, his body rigid with tension from the pain of memories that had not only haunted her, but had haunted him as well. Then Dawn moved closer and softly kissed his brow.

"It wasn't your fault," she whispered, suddenly more distressed for him than for herself. "I know it. I can feel it...even though I can't remember it. I was there, too. You have to let it go."

He clutched her tighter, buried his face in her hair. She felt his great body trembling beneath hers, felt the awful vulnerability of his agony.

Dawn wrapped her arms around him, and he turned into her, clinging, trying to find the strength to go on.

It took him a long time, but finally he told her everything. He told her of the kidnapping, of Mercedes' tragic despair, of his own guilt, of the time they'd locked him up in reform school. He told her that Mercedes had known the true identity of the missing ballerina as soon as she'd seen the necklace Dawn always wore. He described the way Mercedes had hired detectives to dig out every detail of Dawn Hayden's life, how Mercedes had flown to Mexico City herself and spoken to Dawn's adoptive mother.

Mercedes had been horrified by Mrs. Hayden's cold indifference, but from her, Mercedes had learned that twenty years ago Mr. Hayden had found a desperate little five-year-old girl who didn't know who she was, wandering the back alleys of Matamoros. He had brought the child home, forced Mrs. Hayden to accept her and eventually adopted her. Mercedes had gone to New York to see Lincoln.

Dawn listened, absorbing every detail. His words triggered no white flashes. Nothing new came back to her. It was as if he were speaking of someone other than herself, but she was filled with a strange dread.

Kirk swept a mass of hair over her shoulder so that it waved and spiraled against the pillow. "Mercedes never gave up hope, through all the years, that you might be alive. She loves you very deeply."

Dawn felt only an empty nothingness. Only an odd sensation of betrayal. Only fear of an unknown she wasn't wholly prepared to face. "She doesn't even know me."

"She was a ballerina, too. She . . ."

"Please, Kirk, a mother's love is something I'm not sure I can believe in. I know she gave you the money, and you risked your life to save me. I want you to thank her, but I want you to tell her, that for now, I—I don't want to see her."

Thank her! He thought of Mercedes. Of all the years she had suffered not knowing if her only daughter were dead or alive. He understood too well that kind of loss. How would he ever make Mercedes understand that the daughter she had never forgotten wanted nothing to do with her?

"Dawn, the Jacksons are wonderful people, the most wonderful people I've ever known. They stood by me when my own family—"

"Don't you see? New York is all I know. I've fought so hard for my life there. I—just can't go back. Not yet... I'm not her little girl anymore. I don't remember her at all. I would be too afraid..."

Her voice trailed away and they lay together not speaking, both of them numb and exhausted from the wrenching emotional upheaval. Both of them set against each other in this.

Dawn began to sob quietly. "Tell her, please...make her understand how hard it would be for me to go back."

Kirk held her so tightly she could hardly breathe, but the pain in his own heart was as thick and smothering as hers. There was nothing on earth he would not have done for her, so deep were his feelings for her. Who knew better than he how difficult it could be to trust in love? And yet, Jeb Jackson was as dear to him as a brother. Mercedes, dearer than his own mother. Wayne, Nick... Kirk loved them all.

"I don't know if I can find a way to make her understand," he whispered, his voice low with torment.

Then he kissed Dawn and touched her and caressed her until he ignited a wild keening passion in both of them, a passion that brought such joy, that all the pain was blotted out.

The morning was soft and gray and wet. The window was ajar, and sounds from the river traffic sifted inside.

She was on top of him when he awoke, as always. Only this was different. She was softer, more beautiful than ever before, and the erotic feelings she aroused in him were infinitely more tender. Not only the sex, but their talk in the middle of the night, had touched him deeply.

Kirk had meant to get up first and leave her while she was still asleep, but that was impossible now. If he moved, she would awaken. So he lay still and savored the warmth and contentment of their bodies touching, the silken coil of her limbs tangled with his. It was strange how much more enjoyable it was to hold her like this in his arms now that he had made love with her. The tormenting hunger for her was gone, but she seemed infinitely sweeter and more precious.

He understood why she was afraid of going back, afraid of disappointing Mercedes, afraid of finding out for sure she could never go back, that she was truly alone. He knew all about that kind of fear, the fear of opening up your heart. And yet he had to find a way to make her change her mind.

He remembered the long night of passion with a flicker of male pride. How many times . . .

He had lost count. But each had seemed more wonderful than the last. He had wanted her as he'd never wanted another woman, and she'd given herself to him with an eagerness that had astounded him.

No wonder it was so late. He was amazed he hadn't died.

He told himself that he had to break it off, quickly, easily as soon as she awoke.

He lay awake for more than an hour, enjoying the way she cuddled up to him so trustingly in her sleep. Everything about her had become a pleasure to him. Even lying with her when he was wide awake and had a million things on his mind.

When her lashes fluttered drowsily, a terrible sadness gripped his heart.

"Kirk," she whispered, holding on to him.

He looked into her eyes and was dazzled by her beauty and by some indefinable pull of emotion. The time had come for goodbye.

Her fingertip touched his lip, shushing him even before he spoke.

"Stay with me today," she said. "Just one day..."

It was wrong to even consider it, but what was one day out of two lifetimes?

A radiant drowsy smile broke across her face. "Please." With her warm fingertip, she traced the outline of his sensual mouth.

One day with her meant everything, he thought, opening his mouth so that her finger could touch his teeth.

One day meant one more night.

Twenty-four hours to store up a lifetime of memories.

He meant to say no or goodbye, but he heard a rough voice he didn't recognize as his own promise, "Okay. One day."

"And one night," she replied happily, seductively, her expression that of a delighted wanton.

"Who says we have to wait until it's night?"

He nipped her finger and she pulled it from his mouth.

Her eyes were sparkling. "You mean...right now?"

In answer, he lowered his black head, and his tongue traced a burning trail from her breasts to her navel to the warmth inside her thighs, and she cried out.

"Oh, don't touch me. Don't look at me there!" But her fingers were in his hair, pulling him closer.

"I want to touch you, to taste you, to look at you there," he growled.

He could feel her quivering. She arched herself against him with a moan.

God, she was hot. Hotter than any woman he had ever had, and she made him hotter than he'd ever been before.

When it was over she lay in his arms, blushing as she remembered the things he had done to her, the things she had done to him.

Beside her, with her black hair streaming across the glistening muscles of his chest, Kirk was more content and at peace than he had been in years. Her body enchanted him with its exhilarating passion, and yet what he felt for her went so much deeper than sexual desire. Last night when she'd told him softly that she did not blame him for what had happened, that she knew it wasn't his fault she'd been kidnapped and her childhood stolen, he hadn't guessed those lightly spoken words could mean so much to him. But they did.

The sun wasn't shining, but never had a morning seemed more gloriously new and golden. He felt freed of a lifetime of guilt. Even if she wasn't ready to accept her family yet, for him the nightmare was over.

She had freed him. Julia Jackson no longer held him in thrall.

He was free.

At last.

He could go on with his own life.

He thought of Mercedes. Dawn would have to change her mind about that. It was only that the idea of a mother and a family were so new.

He was free.

Never again would he allow anything or anyone to possess him.

Tomorrow he would put her on a plane, and he would be a free man.

The phone rang in the middle of that satisfying thought, and when she didn't move he reached across the beautiful naked woman in his arms and answered it.

"Dawn?" The man's imperious tone was both questioning and possessive, and Kirk bristled.

"She's right here," Kirk drawled, a fierce note of possession in his own voice as he reluctantly handed her the phone.

"Who the hell was that?" both men demanded at the same time.

Lincoln's voice was being blasted into the room by some sort of speaker, so that Kirk could hear every word, and Dawn had no idea how to cut it off. Lincoln could probably hear Kirk as well.

She bolted guiltily upright in bed. "It's just Kirk." Then she glanced toward Kirk who had rolled onto his side and was staring pointedly at the delicious display of her bare breasts, and she blushed. "I—I mean Mr. MacKay, the man who saved me."

"So it's Mr. MacKay now," Kirk said with a contemptuous smirk.

"I mean . . . Oh, hell . . ." She twisted the tail of her sheet into a tangle of wrinkles.

"It's only 7:00 a.m. your time. What's MacKay doing there at this . . ."

Dawn was so used to Lincoln ordering every aspect of her life, that it was a novelty to discover that she suddenly resented it.

Kirk's green eyes blazed. "What the hell does he think I'm doing?" Both men awaited her reply with equal interest.

She clenched the receiver, and her fuming silence was the most eloquent of answers.

"Listen to me, Dawn. I know you're grateful and all," Lincoln began.

"Grateful?" Kirk chuckled. "I'd say that what you felt was a lot hotter and more exciting than gratitude."

"Gratitude has nothing to do with it," she whispered heatedly into the receiver.

"If anyone is asking me," Kirk began, "I'd say it was pure unadulterated lust."

"They're not asking you!" Dawn hissed at Kirk.

"You don't know a damn thing about men," Lincoln's voice thundered. "Especially not a man like him."

"Why don't you tell Mr. Wilde how much you've learned since you last saw him, princess?"

"Would you shut up?" she whispered to Kirk, covering the receiver.

"What?" Lincoln demanded, furious.

"Not you!"

"Dawn, you don't owe that MacKay scoundrel anything. Send him packing. At once."

"He saved my life!"

"He was paid to do it. Tell him goodbye, and get on the first plane back to New York."

"I know you mean well, Lincoln," she replied softly, "but..."

"The hell he does!" Kirk grabbed the phone and slammed it down on the receiver. "Where does that bastard get off telling you how to run your life? He treats you like he thinks you're five years old."

"I'm his dancer."

There was an instant's silence. Emerald eyes touched hers.

Kirk's hand caressed her long beautiful throat. Then he tilted her face so he could inspect it.

"But you're *my* woman," he murmured huskily, his rage gone.

They each seemed to realize at the same minute what he'd said. She felt the hand beneath her chin grow tense. The blood roared in her ears, and she caught a shaky breath. She expected him to back down, but he didn't. His mouth was curved in a tender smile that told her nothing.

"But I thought..." she began.

"So did I," he whispered.

"I thought we weren't ever going to see each other after tomorrow."

"There's no way I can put you on a plane and send you back to that dictatorial jerk and let him push you around. All he cares about is making you dance. The last thing he wants is for you to think or change or grow as a person. He would never encourage you to get in touch with your past. Dawn, you have to come to terms with who you are. Then, if you want, dance."

"No!"

"He wants your body busy so your mind won't be there. If you want to go on as before, fine, but I want it to be your choice, not his."

"You mean..."

Kirk's head moved to the side in a hopeless gesture. "It was my fault you were kidnapped. My fault you've been afraid to live. It's my fault you never had a man...till now. My fault you won't accept who you really are. You've missed so much because of me. I hate the thought of your living the rest of your life like a nun the way that bastard wants you to. I'm taking you to New York myself. Any objections?"

She shook her head, a wild, soaring happiness filling her. "All I know is that I've never felt like this before. I want to be with you as long as I can." She nuzzled her cheek against his throat. "I'm afraid of losing you, afraid of never feeling like this again. I just want to belong to you like this for as long as possible. But when you decide to go...I'll let you."

"Oh, Dawn." He murmured her name in a frantic sigh that seemed almost sad. Tenderly he brushed a strand of hair behind her ear. Then he kissed her, and once he did, he found he could not stop.

A softly muted London sun had come out and was filtering through the damp leaves of the gigantic plane trees of Hyde Park. It was the exact sort of day to be most appealing to Dawn after her ordeal in the desert.

Dawn fitted her foot into the cradle of Kirk's hands, and he boosted her into the saddle.

Frantically she grabbed the horse's mane. "Oops! I told you I've never ridden a horse before."

"You've ridden before. You just forgot."

"I was only five!"

"Just hold the reins, honey." He patted her thigh. "And...relax."

Kirk inspected the horse's tack, then patted the animal's neck, checking everything until he was sure that all was in order. Gently he pulled her foot out of the stirrup and slid his own inside it.

The saddle gave with his weight as his body slid directly against hers from behind. In an instant their bodies were intimately joined in the saddle. His powerful arms reached around her and gathered up the reins. She was aware of every point where his body touched hers.

"How come we couldn't go to an art gallery or a museum?"

"Because you said we could do what I wanted to do, princess."

The horse began to prance, and Dawn jumped, startled. She grabbed at Kirk's hands, and he folded her trembling fingers tightly inside his.

"Easy," Kirk whispered against her ear, "you're going to scare him."

"Scare him! What about me?"

He chuckled. "Remember, you're the one that jumped off the roof and tackled a gang of Arabs single-handedly."

"You know I don't remember that!"

"Nevertheless, you did it. And you can do this. There's only one way to get over a hang-up, and that's to face it head-on. You were crazy about horses when you were a little girl. There's no reason for you to be scared of them now."

He leaned forward and nudged his heels into the stallion's flanks. The giant horse leapt forward.

Every muscle in Dawn's body contracted. "Kirk!"

"Hush. You're perfectly safe. I'm not about to let anything happen to you." Kirk was guiding the stallion out of the stableyard onto a wide dirt pathway.

"Why couldn't you just rent a horse?"

"One of those dispirited nags. No way. I wanted you to get the feel of really riding."

They were on a bridle path with golden sunlight shimmering through emerald-green leaves. There were boats with people rowing on the serpentine lake. The air was cool and damp and filled with springtime freshness, and yet the sounds of the city could be heard.

She began to relax. She'd danced in London dozens of times, but never once had she come to Hyde Park and seen white swans gliding on the lake or ridden on Rotten Row. It was as if London were a new town, and she was seeing it for the first time through different eyes.

"Who does this four-hoofed demon belong to, anyway?" she asked, after they'd ridden in silence for a long time.

"To one of Jeb's friends. In fact, to the powerful gentleman who saw to my release last night."

They passed other riders along the way and drew curious glances from them. Suddenly Dawn became acutely aware of her body sliding up and down against Kirk's in a rhythm that matched the horse's gait.

"Now this isn't so bad, is it?" he whispered.

He was holding the reins with one hand. His other hand was wrapped around her waist.

She felt the heat and pressure of every finger pressing into her. There was possession in his touch. She felt his firm, hard stomach against her spine and shivered. "No. It's really quite pleasant," she admitted breathlessly.

He pulled her closer, adjusting her body to fit his. "I damn sure couldn't hold you like this in a museum."

A ripple of warmth went through her. She laughed. "We'd be kicked out for sure."

Against her ear he whispered. "And I wouldn't want to waste the day doing anything except holding you."

She felt the edges of his fingertips beneath her breasts and hardly dared to breathe.

For a while they rode in silence. They scarcely noticed the beautiful day. They were both too conscious of the way the horse's movements jogged Kirk's taut body against the softness of hers, of his hand holding her tightly to him. She wanted to savor every moment of closeness with him.

"Try to remember when you rode before," he whispered.

"I—I can't."

"Close your eyes," he commanded, "and just let yourself feel it."

She shut out the brilliant day, but when she did, she was aware only of the hot, masculine body aligned against hers, of the thickly muscled thighs and legs touching hers, of the pleasant pervasive scent of Kirk's musky after-shave.

"Nothing," she breathed. She was almost thankful there was no white light, no headache afterward. "I can remember nothing."

"Concentrate!" he whispered fiercely.

It was impossible to think of anything but him. "Nothing. Kirk, I—I . . ." Her voice broke. "Really!"

"Try to remember. You're Julia Jackson, five years old . . ."

She felt the power of the immense animal beneath her. Suddenly the world went white, but this time she managed to hold the flame back. The colors returned, and the sounds. Her head throbbed, and she was terrified.

"I'm not Julia! I'm not! You can't do this to me!" Tears began to course uncontrollably down her cheeks.

"Dawn!" he whispered, reining the stallion to a halt.

She refused to answer him. When he tried to make her turn her head and look at him, she merely lowered her head and sobbed more passionately than before.

He dismounted abruptly and reached up, pulling her down beside him, taking her into his arms to comfort her in her wild grief. Her face was pale, her eyes immense with terror. There was some wall in her mind she was terrified to go past. Never in his life had he felt more guilty of thoughtlessly inflicting pain on another. He was helpless to make amends, helpless to say anything to make her understand that he'd only done what he'd done to help her. She would see it as betrayal. She had told him she didn't want to face her past, and he had refused to listen.

"It's okay, honey," he said soothingly, caressing her arms. "Open your eyes again. There's nothing to be afraid of."

"You shouldn't have . . ."

"I was wrong," he said wretchedly. "I behaved like an idiot. Do you want to go back?"

"Yes," she replied in a flat, cool tone.

In silence, they rode back the way they'd come beneath willows, poplars and elms. A blond spaniel chasing a ball jumped in front of the stallion. When the horse reared, Kirk managed the animal so expertly that Dawn felt only the faintest tremor of fear.

She forced herself to study Kirk's long-fingered brown hands. With expert mastery, one hand had controlled the horse, while the other held the woman. She marveled at the strength and gentleness in those rough callused hands. They knew exactly how to handle a horse, exactly how to touch a woman. She thought of them sliding over her body, caressing her intimately, inflaming her, and she was filled with a wild, tremulous pleasure. He had not meant to hurt her by trying to make her face her past. It would not be so difficult to forgive him for what he'd done.

Much later, when they were back in the stableyard, he helped her dismount, lifting her down so that her body slid against his length.

"I'm sorry," he said again, holding her close.

She tilted her head back. "It doesn't matter. I understand. You were trying to make me whole again."

His sensual mouth twisted. "I did a lousy job."

"It's over." Her eyes were luminous. His nearness sizzled through her like an electric shock. "No one, not ever... No one has cared for me the way you do. You took a risk, but you took it for me. I love you, Kirk. I know you don't want me to, and I don't want to, either. But I do."

She ran her tongue across the pouting fullness of her lips. Then she stretched onto her toes to kiss him. The tips of her breasts pushed against his chest.

Kirk crushed her mouth beneath his and kissed her until he felt the involuntary trembling begin in both their bodies. His fingers crumpled purple silk. Her blouse came loose from her jeans, and she felt his hot hands against her naked flesh.

"I love you," she sighed. The warm moistness of her breath caressed his parted lips.

With languorous slowness his mouth took possession of hers again. "Let's go back to Chelsea."

She opened her eyes and found they would not focus on his face.

"Not yet," she whispered.

The kiss was like a slow burning flame that kept getting hotter and hotter.

"Then where?" he muttered desperately before taking her lips again.

His kiss melted Dawn against his steel-hard body. Her pulse throbbed dully. "A museum," she managed shakily. "Somewhere . . . safe."

At first she thought he hadn't heard her. Then she felt the tensing of his muscles as he slowly became motionless. "I thought you wanted . . ."

"I do." She hesitated. "But now, after baring my heart, I feel like I need some distance. We're so wrong for each other, Kirk. So wrong. And I love you so much."

Her long-lashed eyes lifted and met Kirk's fierce, hungry gaze.

"Whatever you say," he whispered as he reluctantly set her away from him.

The wind was in her loose flowing hair. The smell and sounds of the river enveloped her.

Kirk was at the helm of the boat he had rented to go down the Thames to Hampton Court. The diesel motor of the little boat vibrated as it sped over the glassy waters beneath ancient bridges. Fascinated, like a child, Dawn watched the light glisten in the curls of the following wake.

Kirk glanced at her from time to time, and he thought she seemed vulnerable and feminine and bewitchingly beautiful. The sunlight rippled in her hair; her eyes shone like large ebony pearls. Her face was very expressive and he could read the solemn delight she felt in everything she saw. Silk clung to her breasts; denim hugged her shapely hips and thighs. Why did just looking at her arouse him so?

He closed his eyes and fought to put her out of his mind. Instead, he found himself remembering the way her mouth and tongue had run wildly over his chest and stomach, the way her hand had innocently explored him the night before. He remembered her naked body, and the way it felt beneath his hands. He remembered the hot, sweet taste of her, the joy of that first tantalizing moment when he'd entered her. But most of all he remembered the soft expression on her face when she'd told him she loved him.

He almost groaned aloud at the voluptuous memories. She excited him. It had only been a few hours since he'd had her, but he wanted her all over again. Horseback riding had been a mistake. He had only wanted to help her. Instead, he'd terrified her. He wished she had let him take her back to Chelsea afterward so that he could show her with physical passion what he'd been unable to put into words, that she was right. He cared, more deeply than he should, more deeply than he wanted to.

She was new to sex. An innocent. He couldn't rush her, couldn't expect her to desire him with the same insatiable hunger he felt for her, couldn't expect her to know that sex could be a language between lovers.

He opened his eyes, and the mere sight of her made him ache to take her in his arms. The muscles in his throat tightened. He had to distract himself. He wanted to tell her about the Jacksons, to ease her fears about them, but he chose a safe, neutral topic.

"I'm glad you didn't hold me to the museum," Kirk said dryly at last.

"You looked so unhappy."

Because he couldn't have her. "Lucky for me, you have a soft heart and decided to take pity on me."

"What have you got against museums anyway?"

"I hate closed-in places, cities... I've always lived outdoors."

"We have plenty of museums in New York."

"And I'll bet you've been to all of them," he said, gentle mockery in his deep voice.

"Most of them, but I'm glad we took the boat. I can see museums on any trip. I never get out." Her glance met his, and in his eyes she read some strange emotion. "I'm seeing things I've never seen before," she said in a faltering tone.

"So am I," he murmured, his own voice odd.

"I never realized how beautiful London was," she said dreamily.

"Neither did I." He wasn't looking at the city as she was, or at the river, but at her. He was admiring the way the damp breeze tousled her shining black hair, the way the loose tendrils blew against her rosily flushed cheeks, the way her breasts rose and fell beneath purple silken cloth, the way her waist seemed so narrow about her lushly curved thighs.

She leaned back in the cockpit. Warm sunlight caressed her face. The world floated past. She was feeling things she'd never felt before.

This day had been like no other in her life. The men she had met in New York had always dated her because she was a ballerina, and they had been in awe of her. They liked the status of being seen with a world-famous ballerina. They took her to benefits, openings and galas. She was a dazzling ornament on their arm. She couldn't remember a man ever wanting to spend time with just her, alone. They appreciated her art, who she was, but not her.

Kirk was the first man who had ever treated her as a human being, as a woman. He had skipped the awe and adulation and moved on to something deeper, something that touched some true part of her she'd never known existed. He didn't seem to see her as some glamorous decorative creature in chiffon and lace but as a woman. A real woman that he wanted not only to bed but to know.

She hadn't realized how starved she'd been for something outside the world of dance. She was starved for people, life, thoughts, conversation, for alternatives to her ballet world. For a kind of freedom she had never known. Even though she feared those things.

"So are you looking forward to tomorrow?" he asked, breaking into her silence. "To going back to New York?"

A shadow stole across her face, but she tossed her head with a studied air of nonchalance. "Of course," she said, but her voice sounded uncertain and toneless. For some reason she couldn't look at him, so she looked over the side, deep into the dark brown, swirling waters.

"I suppose New York is the only kind of place for a woman like you," he persisted. "You couldn't ever be happy anywhere else."

She started. "Why do you say that?"

"You're famous. You've made it to the top in a difficult career. Where else are there more opportunities for a person who wants to dance? You have an appreciative audience and a man like Lincoln to guide and shape you...."

She shifted nervously in her seat and tried to force a smile. Suddenly she wished she could turn the clock back so she could relive all the dangerous excitement they had shared together. She almost would have preferred the desert and the thirst, the terrible heat and fear, even the camel, to living without him. She wished she had the courage to face her past.

Kirk was right, of course. Some part of her would always love all the beauty and movement of dance. But would she hate the life that went with it, now that she had known something different? One simply did not throw away years of work, beauty, a job, money and fame... For what? A schoolgirl's dream? A fairy-tale fantasy about true love? Kirk was a man with a life of his own, a life totally different from hers that could never include her.

"Yes, I have to go back...even though I know it won't ever be the same." She sighed. "I'll want more than I had before. Much, much more."

By that she meant a man in her life, Kirk thought. He had awakened her sensual nature, and he doubted she would ever be able to live without sexual fulfillment again. His frown deepened. When he thought of her meeting a man, sleeping with him, Kirk's stomach twisted into a knot. In his jealousy, he imagined some glib cosmopolitan New Yorker who could fit into her world, someone who would take her to museums and art galleries, some paragon who appreciated ballerinas as he never could, and Kirk's fingers clenched the wheel savagely. "It won't be the same for me either, going back to Texas, alone." He hadn't wanted to even think that to himself, much less to admit it to her. Ever.

"But I'll never be sorry," she whispered weakly, desperately, "about anything. Even us... I'll never forget you."

How inadequate—to become nothing more than a treasured memory to her, paling into obscurity as the years passed, he thought.

"Neither will I." But his voice was harsh with pain.

The boat slid beneath a dark canopy of trees, and when it emerged the sun was gone. The colors in the day grayed; the water darkened.

A tension had come between the man and the woman that was almost suffocating, and suddenly they both wished they had said nothing.

But it was too late to take back the words.

Too late to take back the feelings.

The narrow boat drifted lazily down the river toward Hampton Court.

Nine

—

Kirk was tense as he helped Dawn out of the cab in front of the New National Theater of Dance and Ballet. He'd been tense ever since they'd flown into New York the night before. Tense even when he'd stayed with her in that cramped maze of rooms she occupied on Central Park West. Tense even in her twin bed that was so small there had hardly been room for one of them, much less both of them.

She had solved the problem by sleeping on top of him—as always. He had lain awake in the dark, holding her as he listened to the night sounds of a city that never slept, and that might have been his most pleasant time in New York if his thoughts hadn't turned to Mercedes and the rest of the Jacksons.

New York was what Dawn was determined to have instead of them. Kirk was equally determined to show her she could have both. He knew too well what it was to run from the past. She would never be able to be really happy until she accepted herself, everything about herself. It was because of him that she'd been separated from her family. It was his responsibility to restore her to the Jacksons.

The streets and sidewalks were jammed in front of the New National Theater. Kirk glanced up at the theater, at the throng of people on the steps.

It was as impossible to fit himself into her life as it was to fit himself into her bed or co-op. Was there no space—anywhere—for a man to stretch out and breathe in this city? He remembered the shock of her small refrigerator. It had been empty except for diet soda, a can of tuna, juice, seltzer water and cat food. Mostly cat food. When he'd asked about her cat she'd said a friend was keeping it, probably for good as the cat always seemed much happier there.

Kirk had slammed the refrigerator door in disgust and then gone out and bought some real food and cooked a real meal for them both last night. She had laughed at him for stuffing her refrigerator. But she'd enjoyed every bite of the luscious sirloin and potato. And he had enjoyed watching her eat.

"You know I can't cook," she had said.

"Because you never eat."

"I'm too afraid I'll get fat."

"What kind of life is it, when you can't even eat."

"No life at all," she'd whispered. "We dancers live only when we dance."

You're right, he had wanted to say. *No life at all.*

But he had known all along that he could never understand her world.

The crowd rushed past them down the sidewalk in front of the theater. Three men began to fight over the cab as Kirk paid the cabbie.

He had to remember this was her world, not his. This was where she belonged. He wished he could get back in the cab and leave her. Forget her. He wanted to think she would be happy.

He glanced at her and saw her beautiful face frozen with fear as she eyed the waiting crowd in front of the theater. With the desperation in her expression, she seemed so fragile, and he felt intensely protective toward her.

Hell. This place was a jungle. The one thing that would never be possible for him would be to forget her. He had to make sure she would be all right. Most of all, he had to set her free from her past.

Lincoln rushed down the stairs to greet them. A crowd of reporters who'd been waiting for Dawn's arrival swarmed toward them and reached them first.

As a dozen microphones were thrust toward her lips, Dawn seized Kirk's hand and clung to him tightly. "Kirk, this is even worse than I thought it would be. I don't want you to leave me."

"Honey, I'm not going to."

Camera shutters and reporters' questions snapped rapidly in their faces as Kirk forced his way through the crowd and led her up the stairs.

"Miss Hayden, is it true that you're having an affair with the soldier of fortune paid to get you out of Ali Naid?"

"Who paid you, Mr. MacKay?"

"What can a cowboy and a ballerina have in common?"

Speculative glances raked over the powerful man and the tiny woman whose hand he held. A burst of lewd laughter ensued.

"Can we tell our readers the ice princess has a lover at last?"

"I'm from the *Sun*. Miss Hayden, do you plan to return to your career as a dancer?"

"Look this way, Dawn, and give our viewers a big smile."

"Kiss MacKay for us."

A man grabbed Kirk by the sleeve. "Sir, what do you have to say about hijacking that Turkish jet? Who in London pulled the right strings and got you out of jail?"

Kirk's scowl darkened, but to all these questions, he replied tersely, "No comment, gentlemen." He whispered to Dawn. "Just smile. We're almost inside."

Before they could reach the doors, a short fat man grabbed Dawn. "Tell us about your experience as a hostage. What did Aslam Nouri and his men do to you? Is it true that they violated..." The question trailed away luridly.

Dawn blanched, and a wild desperation came into her eyes. What gave him the right to pry into her private affairs? To publish them to entertain his audience?

Kirk seized the little man by his jacket and lifted him onto his toes. "Leave her alone," Kirk snarled. "What kind of man would ask a woman who went through what she did a question like that?"

For an instant the crowd backed away. Frightened by the threat of violence and the dangerous power they sensed in Kirk, a deathlike quiet descended upon the reporters. Then they recovered themselves and began taking pictures, screaming questions more rapidly than before and scribbling notes as Kirk dragged Dawn up the stairs.

Blocking their path, Lincoln accosted the struggling couple. He ignored Kirk and swept Dawn into his arms for a long dramatic bear hug. The reporters closed in on the handsome blond man and his dark-haired ballerina. Dozens of shutters clicked.

Lincoln ran a bronzed hand through his flaxen hair and beamed at the reporters. Obviously he wanted to make the most of this chance for publicity. He thrived on crowds, public attention, on the very things that a man of Kirk's private temperament despised. Lincoln knew that publicity

increased ticket sales at the box office. The kidnapping and
rescue of Dawn Hayden had captured headlines for weeks.

"Mr. Wilde, is it true Miss Hayden left the New National
Theater to dance in Europe and in the Middle East because
she quarreled with you over her career?"

Dawn's face was pale and haggard. Lincoln was beam-
ing. "Absolutely not." He punctuated this lie by flashing his
most gorgeous smile.

"Isn't it true she wanted the part of Beauty in your new
ballet? And that you wouldn't give it to her?"

"The role is hers, gentlemen. Or any other role she wants
for that matter. Miss Hayden is and always has been my
prima ballerina. She will dance Beauty the moment she feels
up to it. Now, if you will excuse me, Miss Hayden is suffering with an injured ankle. She is exhausted."

Lincoln guided her through the doors, and a furious Kirk
trailed silently behind them.

Dawn and Kirk were in Lincoln's lavish corner office suite
overlooking one of the most famous intersections in Man-
hattan. Along the walls were posters and photographs of
famous ballerinas. One of them was Anna Montez. Dawn
tried to avoid looking at the photograph, but she found her
eyes inexorably drawn to it. The resemblance between herself and the dancer was striking.

Her mother's sister... Dawn was both fascinated and re-
pelled. She could not look at the photograph without wondering what her own mother looked like. She could feel the
terror welling up inside her, but she forced herself to ignore
it. Dawn wanted to know about Anna, everything, and yet
she was afraid to know.

"So." Lincoln arched his brows toward Dawn. "You are
back." He fought to suppress his eagerness. "Everything I

told them outside is true. You can have everything you want.''

Dawn's eyes slanted toward Kirk, who was staring silently out the window at the traffic-clogged street below. His hands were jammed into pockets, his great body tense. She wished she knew what he was thinking, what he was feeling, but his dark face was unreadable. She longed to go to him, to let him fold her possessively into his arms, but she didn't dare. He'd been remote, cold, ever since their arrival in New York. It was as if the city itself symbolized all the barriers they were both determined to erect between one another. He was set on her coming to terms with her past. She was set on an opposite path. She no longer knew how to reach him.

Everything? she thought. The brand-new black suit and tie Kirk wore gave him a cultured look, but it didn't conceal the latent power of his body. Nor did it soften the harsh edges of his bronzed face. Her eyes devoured the broad shoulders, the narrow waist and hips, the thickly muscled thighs of the man she loved. A stark longing for something that could never be hers threatened to consume her.

No, dear Lincoln. Not everything... Never again will life be so simple that you can give me everything. I will have to give up something.

"If you'd listened to me and never gone to Ali Naid—" Lincoln began.

She cut him off. "I know. You're right. You always are."

He smiled his most charming smile. "See that you remember that."

She smiled back at him, but now that she was no longer looking at Kirk, hers was a sad smile without enthusiasm.

"You are different," Lincoln said, and for the first time an uneasiness crept into his voice. He too cast a nervous look at the dark brooding figure at the opposite side of the room.

"Anyone would be."

"I suppose so. After what you've been through. And yet it is dangerous for a performer to change."

"Yes. But without change, there cannot be growth."

"You were wonderful before."

"But not wonderful enough to dance Beauty," she murmured.

"A man who is never wrong cannot very easily admit his mistakes," Lincoln whispered. He was his most charming self. "I'm glad you're back."

"So am I," she replied listlessly.

"Without you, there was no one to fight with. Life was too easy. It's good that you left. Now, because of the publicity, you will be a sensation. They will say you're the greatest ballerina on earth. Your heart's fondest dream will come true."

"Yes . . ." She smiled faintly, thinking it odd that she felt so hollow inside.

Pale northern sunlight slanted through the skylights and through the long windows of the studio as Dawn warmed up for her rehearsals. Kirk had been in New York a week. It was Friday, and tonight Dawn was to dance the role of Aurora in *The Sleeping Beauty* to a sellout audience. Afterward Lincoln was throwing a party for the whole company in her honor at his loft. Though Kirk hadn't told her, the Jacksons would be in the audience.

Kirk sat in the shadows watching Dawn's pink toe shoes whirl lightly across the wooden floor, marveling that she could dance with her ankle wrapped. He had watched her pack it in ice, warm it up again, suffer treatments from the sound machine time and time again. It was a chronic sprain, she had told him. She had danced with the pain for so many years, she scarcely felt it anymore.

A dozen girls dressed mostly in pink sat along one wall, sewing ribbons onto their toe shoes for their performance that night, cracking their necks, stretching their toes, braiding their hair as they watched. A few stood at the *barre*. They were thin girls that could do with a man who would feed them a steak or two, pretty girls with smiling, powdered, look-alike doll faces, and all of them were more conscious of him than they were of Dawn.

He wore jeans and boots, a blue cotton shirt open at the throat and a leather bomber jacket. Virile and masculine to the core, he might have felt out of place in such a feminine environment had not all the ballerinas made him feel so welcome. If Lincoln loathed Kirk's constant presence in his theater, the ballerinas spoiled Kirk with constant attention, bringing him cokes, potato chips, cigarettes—these even when he informed them he didn't smoke.

"You have acquired a harem," Dawn had teased, slightly jealous.

"There's more to ballet than I thought," he'd agreed.

"You just like all the pretty girls."

"What man wouldn't?"

"I thought you didn't like skinny girls."

He had just laughed and swept her into his arms.

He must be getting soft, but the week in New York had not made him nearly as crazy as he'd thought it would. Dawn had attended two classes a day and rehearsals; the rest of the time she'd spent with him. He'd gotten into the habit of jogging in Central Park every morning. One afternoon she had taken him out to Montauk where there were wind-swept dunes and boats for hire. On another day, she'd taken him to Fire Island State Park where he'd taught her to fish. Twice they'd taken a train to Connecticut where friends had a house in the country and kept Arabians. Kirk had persuaded her to ride with him again...on her own horse...without openly trying to make her remember her past. Although he tried to make her remember in a thousand little ways.

With every passing day his feelings for her seemed to deepen. The week in New York was the first real vacation Kirk had taken in years.

Once, as Dawn was leaving the theater early, Lincoln had chided her in front of Kirk. "You used to work twelve and fourteen hours a day."

"I will again—after Kirk is gone."

Lincoln's expression had darkened skeptically. "And when will that be?"

Kirk's expression was as grim as Lincoln's. "After she dances."

"She needs to concentrate."

"I need something else—something more than that," Dawn had said quietly, holding onto Kirk. "I'm only following the advice you yourself once gave me."

Lincoln had stalked into a nearby studio.

"I—I'm sorry if he offended..." Dawn had begun.

"Do you think I give a damn about anything he says or does? He's your boss, not mine. As long as you're happy."

"Just don't shut me out. We have so little time," she'd whispered, clutching his hand.

In the studio beneath the white northern light Dawn returned to the *barre* and did *pliés* and *tendus* and stretching exercises. Now that the time was all gone, never had she seemed more beautiful to Kirk. Now that there was no more time to laugh, to love, to make memories.

Tonight she would dance.

Tonight he would leave her.

Never again would he make love to her.

From the *barre*, she glanced toward him expectantly, her face flushed and radiant, and blew him a kiss.

He felt a sudden tearing pain in the middle of his gut, and for a moment his whole being ached for things to be different.

She saw his pain, left the *barre* and danced toward him. He held out his hand to pull her close, and she came eagerly into his arms. Then he kissed her in front of all the other ballerinas, something he had never done before, and as the other girls watched, they felt a jolt of pure envy for Dawn Hayden.

"Vat you thinking about, Dawn?" Sonya cried from the wings, interrupting the dress rehearsal for *The Sleeping Beauty* for the tenth time in less than an hour.

The conductor's baton stopped in the middle of a measure, and Dawn almost fell. Lincoln was scowling darkly at both Sonya and Dawn, but he clamped his lips into a thin line and combed his fingers through his flaxen hair, struggling to say nothing.

His raging silence was more eloquent than words. Dawn knew he didn't want Sonya in his theater any more than he wanted Kirk sprawling in one of the front-row seats watching. Lincoln considered them both interlopers in his own private domain. But for the moment, until he was sure of his power over Dawn, he was going to be lenient with her and let her have her way in such small matters.

Sonya rushed toward Dawn, and Dawn smiled fondly at her slightly eccentric teacher. Though Sonya's long, silvered hair was half hidden by a gypsy scarf, she retained the aura of a Russian aristocrat. As always, she wore her gray leotard, tights and pleated skirt. She took a deep drag from her cigarette holder in desperation. Her once handsome narrow face was lined with age and the sadness that seemed to linger forever in the faces of all dancers who can no longer dance. The sadness was less now, as it always was once she was caught in the passion of teaching her most prized pupil steps that she had once been able to dance herself.

"Take force from your left arm," she said, gesturing with her cigarette holder.

Dawn sailed effortlessly in a pirouette, and Lincoln's scowl deepened because his rival had been helpful.

"Better! Now ven you bend back, let your breath out. It vill be easier."

And it was.

"I remember when I danced Aurora . . ." Sonya began, and her face softened and became lovelier and younger and dreamier.

Dawn always indulged Sonya's sentimental anecdotes.

"You have not danced in years," Lincoln thundered. "You waste time with these stories. We must get on with rehearsal."

Sonya crumpled, and the perpetual sadness in her face deepened into one of her dark impenetrable Russian glooms as she retreated to the wings in defeat.

"Did you have to be so cruel?" Dawn whispered so that only Lincoln could hear her.

"Sorry." He waved his hand carelessly toward the conductor. "I only spoke the truth."

But such a cruel truth. Dawn felt the tragic sadness of her teacher. Was Sonya's present not Dawn's own bleak future? The time would come, too soon, as it did for all dancers, when Dawn's frail body would fail her. Already she suffered chronic pain in her ankle. That would only worsen. There would be new injuries. She would have only a few years, and then she would be the poor, despised creature in

Lincoln's eyes that Sonya was. He would move on to newer, younger ballerinas.

The prospect was hellishly frightening. What would she have then? Who would she be? She might not fare as well as Sonya. Sonya was a realist who'd begun to teach as soon as her career was finished. Dawn knew quite a few dancers who had been forced to stop dancing. Many of them were like lost children without direction, without knowledge, without goals. They had absolutely nothing with which to confront the world of real life. There were sad stories of years of accomplishing nothing, of illegitimate babies, divorces, drugs, breakdowns.

Dawn's eyes sought Kirk's, but she could not see him beyond the glare of the stage lights. Yet she knew he was life, real life. He wanted her to face real life. Suddenly she knew that if she didn't do so now, there would come a day when the reality she faced might be infinitely more grim than the present one. No matter how brilliant her career might be, inevitably it would end. Her energy and ability would be gone. There would be no more limousines, no more galas. Who would want her then?

And yet she was afraid. Some part of her wanted to follow the old pattern of her life and run away into her dreamworld. It would be so easy to lose herself in the hard work and frantic pace of her demanding career.

The music began again, and with it the rehearsal. Dawn began to dance, and though her feet and body performed all the steps and movements with flawless perfection, her heart and soul were depressed and not involved in the process.

"Stop!" Lincoln thundered, utterly exasperated. "What's the matter now?"

"What did I do wrong?"

"Nothing!" Lincoln threw up his hands. "Everything! You know as well as I that it is not enough to dance the steps perfectly. You have to feel them. You have to make the audience feel the passion of the ballet. You know what I felt when I watched you? Nothing!''

"That's what I felt, too!'' she cried, her frustration even greater than his. "Nothing. No spark. I've never felt so empty, like I have no place here, nothing to offer. I'm afraid to dance on stage tonight. I've never been afraid of dancing before, but I am now.''

"It's only stage fright,'' Lincoln said more gently. "All performers suffer from it from time to time.''

"But I never have, and I can't deal with it. You'll have to get someone else. Marguerite, perhaps.''

"The hell I will.''

"Kirk . . .'' Her soft voice was a plea.

Kirk, who'd been watching the entire exchange with dark furious interest, sprang to his feet and rushed up the stairs onto the stage. Dawn flew to him, and he folded her into his arms, holding her so tightly that her pink satin-and-tulle costume was crushed against his leather jacket. The pleasant familiar scents of old leather and his musky after-shave enveloped her. She felt safe, stronger, with him near, with her cheek pressing against the heavy rhythm of his heart.

Lincoln regarded his rival with pure malice. Before Kirk, Dawn had been his dancer. She had wanted nothing but to dance.

"You want her to fail, MacKay. Because you know that's the only way you can have her—if she can't dance anymore.''

For a long moment Kirk said nothing. He just looked at Lincoln steadily, his green eyes suddenly vivid and piercing. At last he said, "And will *you* want her when she can't dance anymore?''

"We're talking about now! This minute! Not some fara-way time in the future! You can't give her anything com-pared to what I can give her—stardom, wealth, fame."

Kirk's arms tightened convulsively around Dawn. "Aren't those the things you want her to give you? You need a brilliant ballerina so people will be dazzled and say Lin-coln Wilde is a brilliant choreographer. All you want her for is your own self-aggrandizement."

"Why you—" Lincoln took a step toward Kirk and then stopped and shifted uncomfortably beneath Kirk's nar-rowed hooded gaze.

The two men were the same size, and yet Kirk's hard body of rippling sinewy muscle seemed infinitely more lethal. For all his talents as a choreographer, Lincoln wisely sensed he lacked the fighting skills a man such as Kirk possessed.

"Dawn needs a break," Kirk said quietly, and yet with complete authority.

"This is my rehearsal. I'm the one who calls for a break," Lincoln hissed.

"Then call one."

Kirk did not wait for Lincoln to do so. He simply led a limping Dawn offstage to her dressing room.

Behind them Lincoln yelled explosively, "Break! Break, everyone!"

In Dawn's dressing room, Kirk held her loosely within his arms for a long while and said nothing. He just stroked her lovely neck and her back soothingly. She thought how pleasant it was to lean against the reassuring beat of his heart. How pleasant it was to have someone stand up for her, just for her with no thought of self-gain. Just this once. These thoughts were followed by one infinitely more treacherous. How pleasant to have this . . . always.

At last Kirk released her, tilted her chin and stared into her eyes. "So, what's wrong? Why can't you dance?"

"I don't know. I just feel scared and unhappy."

"You're the girl who isn't scared of anything," he said gently.

"Oh, Kirk, you're wrong," she said in a voice choked with emotion. "I'm scared of everything. I don't know who I am anymore. What I want."

"Maybe you're scared, but you're the bravest woman I've ever known. Why, you're braver than most soldiers I've fought beside. You saved my life. You endured two brutal kidnappings and survived." He wrapped his arms around her again. "You know something? Lincoln was right in a way. You're not the only one who's scared. I'm scared, too. I'm scared of you dancing because I know it means I'll probably lose you. I'm scared of never feeling like this again for anyone else the rest of my life."

"And yet . . . you want me to dance?"

"Yes."

"Why?"

His gaze moved over her face. "Because I love you."

He started to say something else, but she pressed her fingers against his lips. "Hush," she breathed, her touch feather light. "I want to savor that."

"You must have known."

Gently she touched his bronzed cheek. "But you never said it."

"And are words so important?"

"Very," she whispered, blushing with happiness.

He laughed softly. "Then I love you."

"And what does that mean?" she murmured.

"It means I want you with me always. I want you to marry me. I want you to come to Texas and stay there forever. With your family. With me."

"But you never asked me."

"Because I know you think you belong here."

She bit her lip. "How can you know that, when I don't even know that myself anymore?"

"Dance tonight. For me. Forget Lincoln, the audience, stardom. Just dance for me. More than anything, I want you to be wonderful."

"But, I thought you just asked me to marry you."

"I did. But if you say yes, I want it to be because you want me more than you want this. I don't want you to come to me only because you failed."

"Why, you're an even bigger egotist than Lincoln."

He nuzzled her hair and laughed gently. "Dance for me, darling. Then the choice is yours. Your career, your life here or..."

"Or the man I love."

"So...you said it, too."

"I said it before."

He grinned. "I know." Kirk pulled her closer, and she cuddled against him, her head pressed against the curve of his shoulder. One of her hands moved up to this throat.

"And are the words so important...even to a fierce he-man?"

"Very." He smiled down at her. "Dance for me tonight. For me alone. If I can be brave enough to ask that, surely you can be brave enough to dance."

Confused emotions coursed through her. She saw the same confusion of emotion in his eyes before he enfolded her in a crushing embrace.

"I'll dance," she whispered, "for you."

"Thank you," he murmured against her hair in an odd voice. "I wish—" he began quietly. Then he stopped himself, clasping her tightly, burying his face in her hair, taking in the scent and feel of clean, silken hair and sweet tender flesh, the exquisite sensation of her body fitted to his. "No, the choice has to be yours."

As Dawn clung to him, tears ran freely down her cheeks, whether of happiness or sadness she did not know. She was lost to the world in his arms, oblivious to the rightness or wrongness of her love for him. She was aware only of a thrilling happiness coupled with a soul-numbing sorrow.

She loved him. Tonight she would dance.

Only for this fleeting instant could she have everything.

"Make love to me," she whispered.

She felt him start.

He lifted his head, looking down into her face. "What? Now? Here?"

She touched him in their intimate nighttime way, and his blood ran like fire in his veins.

"Here," she murmured in a soft voice tinged with desire. "Now..."

Ten

Every nerve in Dawn's body seemed to vibrate with tension. She felt hot and cold with dread and anticipation, and it was not only the thought of dancing again that had her on edge. Her whole life was hanging in the balance.

Less than an hour ago Kirk had been in this dressing room with her, undressing her, pulling her down onto the couch, clasping her to his warm, muscled body. She closed her eyes and remembered how tenderly he had caressed her. How hard and callused his hands had felt against her skin, and yet how gently they had touched her. Then his mouth had devoured hers until they were both enveloped in a hot tidal wave of passion.

"Oh, Kirk," she moaned softly. "How can I go the rest of my life without your tenderness? Without your wildness?"

She shook her head sadly and tried to dispel the vision. Then she glanced at her watch. It was six o'clock. The performance was at eight. After rehearsals Kirk had gone home to dress.

Dawn sat with her right foot on a chair, with an ice pack tied on with a pink leg warmer. In front of her was a half-finished cup of coffee, a Tab, an untouched bowl of chicken broth and two pieces of melba toast. Kirk deplored her starvation diet, and he constantly spoiled her with forbidden foods. She nibbled at her deli smorgasbord without enthusiasm while sewing ribbons on her toe shoes.

She could freeze her ankle for only fifteen minutes. To dance on it she would have to thoroughly warm it up. Then after performing *The Sleeping Beauty*, another ice pack.

She had been hard at work on her toe shoes for hours, glad for once of this tedious process. It distracted her from what was worrying her. As always, she had taken her new shoes out of their plastic bags, poured Fabulon into the toes to harden them, cut out the satin toes because they were slippery, pulled out the insoles because they were excess, soaked the toes in alcohol because they were too hard, stepped on them because they were too round, bent the shanks in half because they were too straight, shaved the leather off the bottoms with a rasp because they were too slippery and banged them with a hammer because they were too noisy. She would wear each pair for fifteen minutes of dancing, and then throw them out because the life would be gone from them. Every dancer in the corps used at least twelve pairs a week.

There was a knock on Dawn's door, and her head jerked toward the sound as Kirk strode inside. She gasped.

He was stunning in his black tux with his jet hair tumbling across his brow. As always his brown features appeared chiseled from some dark hardwood. His green eyes were a startling contrast again his dark skin. Even in evening dress, he seemed different from the elegant New York

men she was accustomed to. There was an aura of r⌐
ity about him, a masculine vitality that reached acro⌐
room and jolted her, causing her to tremble visibly.

In his arms he held a lush bundle of blood-red roses.

At the sight of her diet meal, a dark eyebrow flicked up in sardonic mockery. "Starving yourself as always when I'm not around, I see."

"You look wonderful," she breathed. The sight of him was almost a physical pain.

He came toward her and kissed her gently on the brow. "So do you." He separated a single, long-stemmed rose from the bunch and handed it to her.

She caught the fragile sweetness of its scent and gazed up at him thoughtfully. In his eyes she saw an agony of doubt and love that was mirrored in her own.

"Dance for me," he whispered. "Don't worry about the rest. We'll work it out."

She clung to him for a long moment.

Then he was gone.

Oh, why did she feel she'd lost him forever?

Kirk felt a tight, sinking feeling in the middle of his gut as he escorted Anna Montez toward her seat in the rapidly filling theater. Parading behind them down the plushly carpeted aisle were the rest of the Jacksons—Mercedes and Wayne, Megan and Jeb, and Amy and Nick. Kirk was a desperate man, a doomed man running out of time.

He felt that he was being torn between the woman he loved and the family that he loved as dearly as his own.

For days he'd stalled Mercedes with telephone calls.

Half an hour ago at the Jacksons' suite at the Plaza, the entire family had attacked him when he'd come for them alone.

"Where's Dawn?" they had demanded in unison.

"In her dressing room with her ankle packed in ice. She's trying to conquer a case of stage nerves." He'd tried to make his voice light and casual.

"But didn't you tell her we were here?" Jeb said, persistent as ever.

Jeb was the closest thing to a brother Kirk had ever known.

Wishing himself a million miles away, Kirk had shoved thick curtains aside with a trembling hand and stared out the windows at Central Park. "Dawn's not up to dealing with her family yet, Jeb. She's not over the ordeal of the desert."

Mercedes was fighting back tears. "That's what you said last week. Did you even tell her about us? About me?" she had pleaded.

"She knows," came Kirk's grim low tone.

"You mean . . . she doesn't want to meet us?"

Kirk's fingers tightened on a wad of drapes. Hadn't they any idea they were lacerating him with their questions? "Look, I told you she's been through a rough time. The second kidnapping brought back the trauma of the first, and she hasn't been able to deal with her feelings. She doesn't remember . . . anyone."

"You said to give her a week."

"You'll meet her after the performance," Kirk had replied tautly.

Though she said nothing more, Mercedes' eyes had glazed with pain. She was too perceptive not to realize he was holding something back.

The usher flashed a light on Kirk's tickets. "Your seats, sir."

"Thank you."

As Kirk sank into his seat between Anna and Mercedes, he wondered for the hundredth time whether he should have told Dawn the Jacksons were coming.

No. She had been too nervous about dancing as it was.

Still, he felt that by not telling her, he had betrayed her.

Mercedes clutched Kirk's hand, and as he bent his dark head to hers, he cursed his evil luck that he had ended up sitting by her. The last thing he wanted was to hurt her.

"Julia doesn't want us, does she, Kirk? She doesn't want me. That's what you're too kindhearted to say, isn't it? She has her life here, and that's all she wants."

Kirk turned away, a knot in his throat making it impossible for him to speak. He was thankful for the crashing, commanding chords of the overture. It was the theme of the evil fairy Carabosse and the curse she'd put on the ballet's heroine and her family.

With his silence, Mercedes had her answer, and as the music began and the curtain went up, silent glistening tears streamed down her cheeks.

Kirk understood her pain too well. Tonight he was losing the woman he loved, too, as surely as Mercedes had lost her daughter all those years ago.

The haunting drama of Tchaikovsky's music filled the theater, but Kirk did not hear it.

Why did it always have to be this way for him? First his mother, then Julia, the little girl he had adored. Then his father. Would it always be his fate to love and lose? Why couldn't he have fallen in love with some rancher's daughter from Texas? Someone who didn't even know there were such things as tutus and pink satin toe shoes?

The violent music was interrupted by a melodious harp, which introduced a soft, slow, magical, compassionate theme—the melody of the Lilac Fairy, whose beauty and goodness would triumph over the evil fairy's challenge.

Though Kirk said nothing, his large hand closed over Mercedes' as if he sought to impart his strength to her.

Lincoln's version of *The Sleeping Beauty* was magnificent. The muted grandeur of the setting was calculated to give prominence to the dancers, and the costumes had all the splendor one could want without any exaggeration of color or proportion.

Dawn danced Aurora as never before. For was it not her own story, the story of lost years, of living in a dark dreamworld, of being cut off from one's real life? Oh, why was it so much easier to assume the identity of a make-believe character and dance than it was to live one's life in the unpredictable wilderness of a too-real, unchoreographed world? Why was it so much easier to be Aurora, awakening to real life and true love, than to be herself and do the same things offstage?

The curtain came down after the last act to the thunder of applause. Everyone in the audience leapt to their feet and clapped. Kirk got out of his seat, went quickly backstage, picked up the bundle of flowers he had brought Dawn and gave them to Lincoln to take to her.

Dawn was breathless from the last mazurka, but on her fifth curtain call, she beckoned to Kirk. He pretended to ignore her by skulking behind a curtain, but she came after him and dragged him reluctantly on stage where she handed him a rose from her bouquet. She looked at him, smiling shyly, and blushed radiantly. It was a public gesture of her love for him, and the audience clapped more wildly than ever before.

Even Lincoln was pleased. Tomorrow the cowboy, and the ballerina he had rescued from Arab terrorists, would again be a hot news item. Everyone would demand to see Dawn dance, and that would mean increased ticket sales.

The stage lights blinding him, Kirk's cheeks darkened. His tense body froze, and he crushed the rose between his taut brown fingers. Dawn had meant to show Kirk how much she loved him, but what she'd shown him instead was how different they were. She was a creature of light and dazzle, of fame and fortune. He was a private man, a man uncomfortable with such a public display of devotion. Grimly, for her sake, he endured the spotlights and the deafening applause.

Dawn received numerous curtain calls, and every time she came out from between the rich black velvet folds of cloth, the audience went wild, whistling, cheering, clapping.

And every time that happened, Kirk felt something vital and precious in his chest withering and dying.

Dawn's dressing room was jammed with flowers, telegrams and elegant people. Most of all with laughing, shouting, smoking people who wanted to bask in the limelight of Dawn's glamour and success. They were Lincoln's friends, wealthy patrons who supported his theater.

Dawn could hardly endure their compliments. She wanted Kirk, only Kirk, and the warmth and strength of his comforting presence, not these strangers with their artificial smiles, not these people who surrounded her only because contact with someone famous gave them an emotional high, not these rich mothers all vying for pairs of her autographed toe shoes for their little girls. Kirk didn't care about her fame or her ballerina aura; he cared only for her, for the woman she was. It was ironic that on her greatest night of triumph as a dancer, never before had she longed so fervently to be only a woman. But Kirk had vanished the moment he'd managed to escape.

Behind the facade of her glamour, Dawn was in an agony of physical pain. Her toes were bloody and aching and wouldn't point; her ankle swollen as always. She wanted to remove her stage makeup, pack her ankle in ice, put on something more comfortable than her glittering white-and-gold costume and spend the rest of the evening alone with Kirk. But in an hour, Lincoln was throwing his party in her honor.

In the corner Lincoln was giving an interview to a reporter.

"The dancer, no matter how wonderful, is never more than an instrument of the gifted choreographer. I am forced to work with dancers, each of whom has a distinctive will, personality and a set of performing characteristics. Some of the most wonderful dancers are the most difficult."

"And Miss Hayden?"

At Lincoln's hesitation, a hush fell upon the room.

"She is one of the most wonderful."

"And one of the most difficult?"

Another little sensitive silence, as Lincoln merely ran a brown hand through his flaxen hair, raised his brows and smiled benignly.

Dawn flushed, and Lincoln's audience laughed quietly.

Dawn dug her nails into her palms. Dancers meant nothing to Lincoln beyond their usefulness in his artistic medium. She was not even a person in his eyes. Just an instrument. Necessary to him. Something to be endured despite limitations. When Dawn could no longer dance, he would find some younger dancer with her own distinctive will.

Where was Kirk? Why hadn't he come? He had seemed so grim on stage when she had given him the rose to show him how much she loved him. His body had felt alien and tense when she'd tried to touch him. But surely he would not leave her without saying goodbye. Surely... Didn't he know how much she needed him? Now more than ever?

Since he hadn't come to her, the darkest terrors of her imagination overpowered her rational mind.

Blinking to keep back tears, Dawn rose from her seat and hobbled through the throng, intent on finding him.

She stepped out into the dark hall, and there he was, standing in a pool of light. She would have rushed toward him, but he was not alone. Two lovely, older, dark-haired women, a matched pair in glittering jewels and dark evening gowns, clung uncertainly to his arms. With them also was a silver-haired man and two handsome younger couples.

Instantly Dawn recognized Anna Montez, though she was older now than in the picture in Lincoln's office. Dawn's gaze left her aunt's face to rest on Mercedes'.

There was a nightmarish unreality about the moment. A dazzle of blinding whiteness suddenly made it difficult for Dawn to see, impossible for her to breathe.

But surely that gently lined face framed with dark hair was the sweetest and dearest on earth. Dawn felt the woman's dark, luminous eyes, so like her own, fasten on her face, upon the golden medallion against her throat.

Dawn's shaking fingers went to the gleaming pendant. Mother...

"You're alive," Dawn whispered in strangled disbelief. "Alive... I thought..." She had no idea that she had spoken out loud. The back of her head was throbbing. The world whitened.

She swayed forward, but her feet didn't move.

It was the face she dreamed of every night and yet forgot every morning that she had. It was the face she had blocked out of her mind because it was too belovedly painful to remember.

Her mother's face dimmed and whitened as the intense light consumed everything in its blistering flame. Dawn's head pounded with some ancient forgotten terror.

Far away, she heard the sound of someone screaming. The world seemed dreamlike, unreal, separated from her by a shield of black glass.

A child was crying in the night for her mother; crying in a night that never ended for a mother who never came.

Dimly, Dawn realized she was that child.

In a single blinding flash, her memory of that awful time came back to her. She remembered not only the things Kirk had told her in London, about the men coming to the ranch and kidnapping her, but the terror of that time afterward.

She'd been locked in a dark trunk, and then a dark closet, for countless days and nights until she'd thought she'd go mad from the darkness. All she had thought of was her mother's face. All she had dreamed of was her mother coming, of her mother miraculously finding her somehow and saving her.

The men had laughed cruelly at her tears and taunted her. "Your mother's dead. She doesn't love you. You will never see her again."

At first Dawn hadn't believed them. Then they'd gone away and left her all alone in the dark, telling her not to try to escape, that they were coming back. Somehow she'd gotten out and gone to look for her mother, but she'd never found her. Dawn had been lost and afraid, more afraid than she'd been even with the kidnappers.

Slowly she'd come to believe the men's words. Her mother hadn't loved her, hadn't saved her. Her mother had betrayed her. Then Dawn, the child, had buried that agonizingly painful knowledge safely inside herself and begun the arduous task of starting her life over with strangers.

In the dark hallway, Mercedes' lovely anguished face seemed to spin at the center of a dizzying whirlpool of light and pain. Dawn wanted to reach out to her, but she lacked both the strength and courage.

Dawn was fainting, dying. Her heart seemed to be bursting in two.

Dawn wanted her mother. She didn't want to want her mother. It hurt too much to want. And never to have. She clawed the air like a sightless person and tried to reach her. She was only vaguely aware of strong arms subduing her.

Slowly the awful sensation receded, and she came back to the present. She was wrapped tightly in Lincoln's arms. Her dark head was pressed into his shoulder as if she were attempting to shield herself from some terrible danger. A dark, greasy smudge of stage makeup was smeared on his white dinner jacket, but his golden features were gentle, yet grimly concerned.

She felt a terrible weakness, a breathlessness at the center of her being, a guilt settling into her spine like melting lead. Kirk was leaning over her, his dark face anxious, but she was cringing away from him, sinking more deeply into Lincoln's protective arms.

"Dawn," Kirk began, "I want you to meet..."

For a second longer Dawn focused on her mother's beautiful face. Then it blurred in the thick veil of her falling tears.

Dawn's breath wouldn't come. She couldn't speak. The shock was too great. She had to have time. More time. Once again, as he had that first time in Hyde Park, Kirk had deliberately betrayed her.

Despite her attempt to pull away, Kirk took Dawn's cold white hand and held it in his warm one. She felt the hard edges of his silver bracelet biting into her skin. He was silent, watchful.

"Maybe I shouldn't have brought them," Kirk said, "but you had to meet them sometime."

The medallion lay like a heavy cold weight upon her throat. Dawn tried to speak but managed only a strangled sound.

"They're your family," Kirk whispered. "I know you said you can't go back, but you have to. Or you can't go forward."

Some part of her knew that he was right, and that knowledge frightened her more than anything. She wasn't their lost little girl anymore. She had been on her own for years and years. What if they didn't want her anymore?

Your mother doesn't want you...doesn't want you... Like a hypnotic chant, the kidnapper's words chimed in her head.

Why couldn't she do something? Say something? Why did she feel paralyzed? Like she couldn't go forward, no matter how she wanted to? Like she was locked in her past, imprisoned inside herself?

Perhaps it didn't matter so much that she couldn't reach out to them, she thought. Loving meant accepting the frailty of that love, accepting all the doubts, all the risks, all the hurt. Maybe she'd been hurt too deeply to ever do that again. Maybe she was not the same brave little girl they had lost. Maybe she could never be whole. Never be the person they wanted her to be. Maybe they deserved something better, something finer than she could ever give them. Something whole. She was a sham. She could only appear whole when she was the glittering creature of some dream of Lincoln's creation. But never in real life. Maybe she belonged in New York. On stage.

She sensed that Kirk was judging her; that she was failing some vital test.

"You told me to dance for you," she whispered, frantic.

"You were wonderful," Kirk said.

"No one was ever more so," Lincoln agreed proudly. "Tonight was a triumph, unlike any in your career. A turning point."

"Yes," she murmured helplessly.

"You are a great artist," Lincoln said. "You will be the greatest ballerina in the world. After tonight there can be no going back."

She turned from Lincoln to Kirk and felt pulled between her two lives. "Kirk, you said I could choose what I wanted, if I danced."

She felt the hard pressure of his warm fingers on her hands.

"Yes," came his low hoarse whisper, a desperate sound.

Behind him stood the Jacksons, poignantly regal in their silence.

How could she ever fit into their lives without disappointing them? It seemed to her that some powerful barrier of will separated her from tnem. Some ancient terror that even now was all-powerful.

"You know nothing of Texas. You hate horses, the country, the heat. You're a city girl, a New Yorker, like me," Lincoln said. "They would never understand you, any more than you could understand them. This is where you belong."

"This is where I belong," Dawn echoed mechanically in a small bewildered tone.

Kirk flushed angrily. "You can't let him choose for you without even saying a word to your family," Kirk ground out, his patience snapping like a taut wire.

Dawn could feel Kirk's rage quivering in his voice; she could feel the same intense emotion shaking in his hot hands that cut into hers.

A soft voice from behind him said firmly, "She has chosen, Kirk. Let her be."

The softest, sweetest voice on earth, Dawn thought. Her mother's voice, part of her sweetest, dearest, most tender memories. Dawn longed to go into her mother's arms, to be the lost little girl returned to her mother. But the bitter truth was that she could never be that little girl. Mercedes' little girl had been lost forever.

Dawn couldn't meet Kirk's gaze, but she smiled brilliantly, bravely. Her stage smile.

Vaguely, she was aware of his face slowly hardening into a cold, aloof mask, of his slow determined withdrawal.

Dawn could not tell him that she loved him more than anything on earth. That she needed him. That she needed her family, too. That she needed her mother. That she didn't understand the force inside herself that made her hold back.

She was aware of Lincoln's eyes blazing with a mixture of triumph and exhilaration as he lifted her to her feet and led her back to her dressing room, back to her world, before she gathered her wits and changed her mind.

"You will have everything you have ever wanted," Lincoln promised her.

She felt empty and alone among the glittering throng of wealthy ballet patrons. Not cool and safe and remote as she'd thought she'd feel.

She touched the glimmering, fiery pendant of the sun that lay against her throat. For once she found no courage in touching it, only pain. Its ragged metal edges cut into her skin like knives of ice.

"Yes, everything," she whispered. "Everything..."

But even as she said it, her heart was shattering into a million pieces.

On a desperate impulse, she ran out to the hall to call Kirk back, but he had already gone.

"Let him go," Lincoln said. "It is for the best."

Eleven

In white chiffon, Dawn was elegant, ethereal, ghostly—lost. The sounds of laughter and gaiety enveloped her.

Tonight was the moment of her greatest triumph, but she felt only a profound and bitter despair.

She had everything.

But without Kirk, without her family, it meant nothing.

Why had she run from love?

Because she had not known the cost.

There are some decisions one cannot know are wrong until they are made.

For years she had survived by cutting all feeling from her life so that she would never be hurt. But Kirk had come to Ali Naid and saved her, and she had fallen in love with him. She had let herself feel, and she could not stop, even though now all she felt was pain.

It was not so easy to go back, to live the life she had once led, to turn herself into a talent machine for Lincoln, to live without hurt, to live without the knowledge that she was hurting others.

Tonight, by denying her true, terrifying feelings, she had betrayed her own mother as well as the man she loved. Because of her, they too were suffering. Real life was not simple.

Misery seemed to close in upon Dawn like suffocating walls of darkness.

Not that Lincoln's party wasn't fabulous. It was an extravaganza with its buffets overflowing with caviar, salmon, cheeses, fruits, breads, pasta. With its endless lengths of rare filet mignon and bubbling champagne. With its live rock band—and a crowd in one corner dancing wildly.

The large white rooms of the Wilde loft were filled with expensive furnishings, expensive food and expensive people. The guests were brilliant, ambitious, talented or, at the very least, merely wealthy. Then there were the dancers.

The dancers, in their gold threads, gold sparkles, gold socks, gold hair clips and brightly mixed purples, pinks and reds, stood out from the crowd because of a certain outrageous wacky behavior. Their humor was physical and filled with mimicry. Marguerite was enacting a parody of Aurora for an enraptured audience.

Dawn made no attempt to participate in the festivities. She was a ghost who could not fit into their vital world. All she could think of was the pain in Kirk's eyes, the pain and love shining in her mother's face, and Dawn knew she had caused that pain. Why had it seemed so frightening to face her family? Why had she run?

She had lost everything she really wanted by running. Suddenly, as she looked about the glittering party, she felt lonely, as if she did not belong here, as if she never would again. Her glamour was a facade that only made her loneliness worse.

She was filled with a terrible emptiness, the way she always was after she danced. One put in all one's energy, time and soul into a performance, then it always ended, every night. In a few years it would end for good. She was building nothing that could last, nothing that could mean anything. Her life would be filled with endings if she stayed in New York. Nothing more.

She wanted Kirk, her family, her mother. Dawn had always run from life, but that was before she had known who she really was. The second kidnapping and all that had followed had slowly caused her to regain her memory. She did not have to hide from her past anymore. It was part of her, something she had to accept.

Seeing her mother had been such a shock, Dawn had not known what to do.

Suddenly she knew that she had to find her mother, that she had to find Kirk as well.

In a daze, Dawn stumbled toward the door. Surely they were still in the city somewhere. She would call every hotel until she found them. Surely it was not too late to make up for what she had done.

She was halfway across the room, when drums began to thunder and a strobe light flickered on. She whirled, frozen for a brief second in the flashes of light. Lincoln came to her, swept her into his arms and spun her around in a wild dance. Lincoln was a superb dancer, and they always danced together once at every party. She started to resist him, but then decided it would be rude of her to reject him publicly.

All the guests shrank against the white walls to watch the mesmerizing couple; the tall golden man and the small dark woman. She let the savage jungle beat become a part of her. Her graceful body twirled sensuously, rhythmically, and she turned her emotional anguish into wild, passionate, beautiful movement. Her hair came loose and flew in silken waves against her neck and shoulders. Her gauzy skirts circled high above her knees to reveal her shapely legs.

As always, when she danced, she was the most electrifying presence in the room. No man or woman could take their eyes off her.

The door opened, and a tall dark man in evening clothes entered just as the music built to a throbbing crescendo. Dawn threw her head back so that her hair swung like a black veil over her white gown. Lincoln effortlessly lifted her in his arms and carried her high over his shoulders so that her chiffon gown glowed over his arms.

Lincoln was laughing as he set her down, and something he said caused Dawn to laugh, too. They seemed caught up in the tempo of the music.

Kirk brought his hand down, flat on the surface of a table, like the blade of a wide sword. Champagne glasses jumped; large wet pools stained snowy linen beside the glasses.

Dawn stopped dancing and began to tremble as Kirk stormed through the crowd, his dark face livid with anger and some other unnameable emotion. Green eyes blazed through Dawn and made her feel naked with guilt.

In two strides he crossed the room, grabbed Dawn's wrist and snapped her against his hard body.

The music stopped. Lincoln's golden face contorted. Everyone gasped and watched spellbound.

"Sorry, folks," Kirk drawled into the stillness and silence. He was as mesmerizingly charismatic as Dawn. There was not a woman in the room who did not shiver. "The show's over."

Then he took Dawn's unresisting hand and pulled her across the emptiness in the center of the room toward the door. There was not a woman in the room who would not have gladly gone with him.

"What the hell do you think you're doing?" Lincoln yelled, outraged.

"Just get out of my way!" Kirk barged past him, pulled her out the door, out into the hall, down the stairs.

"Kirk, what's wrong?" she whispered, stumbling, terrified.

"The fact that you have to ask," he snarled, pausing on the landing and shoving her against the wall. "How can you be so blind, so selfish? How can you turn your back on your own people?"

"I—I wasn't going to. I was coming to find you."

"Sure."

"I was."

He was rigid. She felt the power of his eyes, his anger.

"I don't believe you, Dawn. That was quite a performance back there."

"I love you," she whispered desperately. "I want to be with you for the rest of my life."

"In Texas? Living with me on a remote ranch? Raising horses? Having children? The hell you do. You chose Lincoln and what he can do for you. Parties. Dancing. Fame."

"If you hate me so much, then why did you come back?" Her voice was bleak, tired, frightened.

"Not for myself," he muttered coldly. "Because for once in your selfish life, you're going to do something for someone else. Mercedes collapsed when she got back to the Plaza. Oh, she was strong for you, but that was just an act. She waited twenty years to get her child back. She never gave up the belief that you were alive. She sent me to Ali Naid with a million dollars to get you out. I risked my life for her . . . because of you, and damn it, you're going to talk to her and pretend that it means something to you."

"It does."

"Hell." The single word held dry contempt.

In one swift motion he jerked her closer to his body. "Why do you have to be so beautiful?" Gently his fingers traced the soft curve of her cheek. "So desirable that you make me hate myself because I can't stop wanting you. Because I can't stop loving you."

She felt the heat of him, the rage and the desire.

He leaned into her until her legs were glued against his muscled thighs, her breasts pressed against the solidness of his chest. She tried to fight him, but it was no use. He was too furious, too determined. The blistering heat of his lips claimed hers. She felt his tongue stroke insolently across her lips and slide deep inside her mouth. She went limp in his arms.

Despite his savage anger, she wanted him to kiss her; oh, she wanted him, more than she'd ever wanting anything. She felt she would die if he didn't kiss her. She loved him, and she'd hurt him. And it was killing her as much as it was killing him. She had to find some way to make him understand that he was wrong. That she was sorry. That she hadn't known herself. That she'd never never wanted to hurt him or the Jacksons. That without him her life would be over.

His mouth ground against hers, and the flame inside him ignited an answering flame in her. A quivering started deep in her belly and worked its way down her thighs, causing an aching, pulsing desire. Her arms went around his neck, and her mouth trembled beneath his.

As abruptly as he'd seized her, he pushed her away, and she fell back against the wall, breathless from the passion a mere kiss so effortlessly aroused. Her mouth stung, and she traced her hand across it. His brilliant eyes studied her face, followed the path of her fingertips across her lips.

Every female nerve in her body clamored in awareness of him.

"You're very good." There was a curl to his lip. "Very good at getting next to a man, at making him want you." He twined his fingers in the loose strands of dark hair and turned her face closer to his. "Did you feel anything? Or was I just amusing? A cowboy lover? A good time—for a while?"

"Don't destroy our love," she pleaded.

His laughter was tinged with a savage bitterness. "What love? You don't know the meaning of the word."

Dawn paled, and he caught her by the hand once more and pulled her down the stairs, outside and into a waiting taxi.

All too soon she was outside the door of the Jackson's suite, desperately clutching Kirk's arm, which was as hard and steady as granite. Her pulses were pounding with fear. He hadn't said a word in the cab, in the elevator.

The door was opening, and Kirk was pushing her inside, not following.

She was surrounded by her family.

Never in all her life had she felt so alone.

"Kirk..."

She turned toward him, but he would not even look at her. He pivoted on his heel and disappeared down the hall, into the elevator.

He was going. Walking out of her life, and she knew of no way to call him back.

She stepped uncertainly inside the hotel room. A blazing white light seemed to fill it. Everyone was frozen, even the weeping woman on the bed. There was an odd hush, a terrible stillness that caught at Dawn's heart.

Her family couldn't believe she had come.

Kirk was leaving her. She fought against the agony of light.

But she was coming home.

She wanted to run, to cry.

A crushing, unbearable pain weighted her heart, and yet there was joy, too.

She stared at them all wordlessly—her brothers, both tall, one golden, one dark like herself, her father.

Then through the brilliant diamond light, the fragile woman on the bed arose and came slowly to her. Dawn stood still, afraid to move forward, afraid that this woman who seemed to be her mother was a mere fantasy of her desire.

Mercedes' black eyes shone with a feverish certainty and courage. Slowly, wonderingly, gentle maternal arms enfolded a long-lost child, a woman now.

The pleasure and rightness of touching the body that was, indeed, her mother's sang sweetly in Dawn's veins. Tentatively, she slipped her hand around her mother's waist and clung. She felt her mother's tears falling against her own cheeks. The familiarity of her mother's scent enveloped her. She had come home. At last. She was loved. At last. Truly loved.

"I never gave up, *querida*," Mercedes murmured in her small, clear voice. "I always knew you were alive."

"I'm not your little girl anymore..."

"You will always be my little girl, *querida*. Always."

Dawn felt the pull of something right and pure, something that went beyond loss and unshared years. She began to weep too.

How odd it was that the comfort of her mother's body, so well-known, so deeply loved, could have been forgotten.

Dawn felt that she had stepped out of cold darkness into fragrant sunshine and summer air. The bitterness and loneliness of years was washed away.

A girl with red hair and luminous green eyes came to her. "Julia, I'm Megan, Kirk's little sister. Your brother Jeb's wife."

"I remember you. We used to play together when we were children."

Gently Megan touched Dawn's hand. "If Kirk hadn't found you, if he hadn't gotten you back, he would have kept on risking his life going after other kidnap victims. One day his luck would have run out, and he wouldn't have come home. Now I won't ever have to be afraid again."

Dawn smiled wanly.

She was glad he had brought her home and forced her to accept her family. She was loved, wanted, accepted.

But it wasn't enough.

She remembered Kirk's savage bitterness, and she felt an aloneness worse than anything she had ever known. With eyes glazed over with ice, he had walked out on her—forever.

Even with her mother's arms tightly around her, even with Megan's love shining in her eyes, Dawn's heart ached with an utter despair, with a fear that went all the way to her soul.

Twelve

—————

The red, dust-coated jeep bounced along a dirt road. Dawn still wore her white chiffon dress from the day before. She had left all the Jacksons at the Big House so she could look for Kirk.

Dawn was afraid, not of driving, though she'd lived too long in a city of taxis and subways to be very good at it. She was afraid of facing Kirk in his house alone, of not being able to find the words to make him believe that she couldn't live without him. He was so proud, so terrifyingly proud.

A brilliant sun was dying in a purple sky as Dawn stopped the jeep and got out to unlock the gate. For an instant she savored the spacious emptiness of the warm, vast land that stretched endlessly to far horizons.

Home. She had come home.

She felt a sense of belonging that she had never felt in New York. Never felt anywhere else. She had loved the great Jackson house. The Big House. Loved this empty land of cactus and mesquite and oak, been part of it, been brutally taken away from it.

Slowly she got back into the jeep and drove it with a rumble across the cattle guard and left the gate swinging open in the cloud of dust behind her. She shot past meadows of bluebonnets and Indian paintbrush.

Would Kirk be home? Would he be so stubbornly set against her that he wouldn't even listen to her? Would she have everything but the man she loved?

Two miles down the road, the MacKay ranch house was as she remembered it from her childhood. It was a house with clean, simple lines, with wide verandas on every side, a freshly painted house nestled in a shadowy grove of salt cedar and gnarled live oak. The blades of a windmill sang pleasantly, groaning in a faint breeze, and the whining sound filled her with a sweet nostalgia. Jeb had told her that Kirk had bought the MacKay Ranch back from him with his gas royalties, and that he had remodeled it and moved into it several months before.

Dawn stepped cautiously onto the porch. Curtains billowed against screened windows, and she could see into the rooms. In the bedroom there was a large bed with a brass frame. A man's leather jacket was carelessly flung across the quilted spread. The television was on in the living room, and a beer bottle sat tipped at a queer angle beside a leather chair, as if Kirk had set it down in a hurry and gone somewhere.

Dawn could hear Kirk in the kitchen. She caught the scent of coffee brewing, the smell of warm bread and a steak baking in a hot oven.

Was that the only thing he knew how to cook? She would have to learn to cook herself so she could vary his menu.

She pushed the screen door open and stepped from darkness into the softly lit room.

It was a comfortable house, though sparsely furnished. A rifle lay against the fireplace. A box of shells was open, and some of them had spilled onto the floor. It was the house of a man. She would change that, too.

The door closed soundlessly behind her, and she knew that she belonged here and nowhere else.

"Kirk..."

He heard the velvet sound and came to the doorway. The light came from behind him, and his immense body was framed in its radiance. He was shirtless, in his jeans and boots. Golden light splashed across powerful male muscle, and she felt her pulse quicken. His silver bracelet gleamed against his dark wrist. He stood perfectly still, looking at her.

The wind blew through the screens, blew her hair about her neck and shoulders, blew the filmy chiffon about her slender form. She could feel his eyes burning across her face, over her body.

Then he walked slowly toward her, his boot heels echoing on the wooden floors. His handsome face was gentle yet haggard, as though he hadn't slept at all, as she hadn't during the long hours that had separated them. He stared at her, his gaze filled with doubt until at last he saw her love for him shining in her luminous dark eyes.

"Don't send me away," she whispered, reaching toward him. "Please."

She touched his arm, and he felt as hard and unyielding as a statue. Yet he was hot; not a statue at all. She was afraid as she'd never been afraid.

After an agonizing length of time he folded her into his arms.

"As if I could," he whispered on a hoarse, ragged note, burying his face in her hair.

A sob caught in her throat.

"I never thought in my wildest dreams...you'd come here," he said.

"I never want to be anywhere else."

"What?" He stared at her, stunned. "Leave New York? For good?"

"It's only a city."

"It's much more than that. It's your life. It's everything."

She reached up to touch his cheek with trembling fingers. "No. You're my life. You're everything."

"I love you," he said. "More than I've ever loved anyone." There was both agony and joy in his voice as his arm tightened and crushed her to him. She felt him shaking with intense emotion, and she began to tremble as well.

He did not ask her again what she was doing here. He believed her.

She kissed his face, and he began to laugh. His large hands spanned her tiny waist. Slowly he lifted her high above his head and let her slide down once more against his body.

"You're light as a feather," he murmured.

She smiled, pleased.

"That wasn't a compliment," he said huskily.

"To me it was. I like being skinny."

His hand moved beneath the silken mass of her dark hair. His palm traced the curve of her breast. "I'm going to change that."

"You can try," she whispered.

The laughter died in his eyes, and for a long moment he was silent. "Are you sure?" Again his tone held anguish. "Can you really give it all up?"

Her breasts rested against his hot, muscled chest. Dawn felt a simple physical happiness that just being near him gave her.

"I missed you so much," she said in answer, knowing that she couldn't live without him, couldn't live without his voice, without his body. Without him. "It means nothing to me . . . without you."

He took her fingers and kissed them, one by one.

The air was heavy with the smell of cooking. The steak was sizzling and popping.

"Dawn! I forgot the damn steak! I'd better turn the stove off," he cried, taking her by the hand and rushing her into the kitchen, "before I burn the house down."

Swiftly he turned off the oven. He smiled at her, a smile that was so warm and exciting that she dared not look at him for too long. When she kept looking at the floor, he ran his callused finger lightly along her delicate jawbone. "We'll eat later," he said softly.

Outside the screened kitchen windows, the too-early darkness of the range and the afternoon smelled fresh and sweet. Someday soon he would teach her the individual smells of jasmine and climbing roses and huisache and mesquite. And all the wildflowers, too. But not now. Not now, when her presence was like a living thing heating his blood.

His fingers tightened on hers. Inside the house, the air was charged with the jet of their sexual excitement.

He led her into the bedroom and turned off the light, holding her quietly in the darkness. Slowly he pulled her down beneath him on the bed. Laying his face tenderly against her, he kissed her over and over.

She stroked his cheek. Then she traced the hard muscles of his chest and shoulders with her eager hands.

All that dark night, she would have him to herself.

For all the rest of the dark nights in her life, he would be hers.

And she knew that never again would she be afraid of the darkness, because he would be with her, holding her, loving her—forever.

He would be her husband, the father of her children. Her life. Everything.

The future stretched before her like a dazzling light. A warming brilliance—no longer a terrifying one. It was a blazing happiness that would fulfill her completely and last forever.

"Say my name," she whispered.

"Dawn."

"No! My real name!"

"What?"

"Say it," she pleaded. "Call me Julia." Her light, yet urgent, tone drifted away in the darkness.

She felt his hands go still in her hair. For a long time he was silent.

"Julia," he said very slowly, very reverently. "My darling Julia."

Though his mouth closed gently over hers, she could feel his desperate passion, his wild elation, the tornado whirling inside him.

Tenderly, insistently, his hand flowed downward, warm, slow, but sure, touching her everywhere, arousing her, claiming her, making her his.

He lifted his head, looking down into her beautiful face.

"Julia..." His voice was husky, uncertain. "Darling."

Her eyes sparkled with unshed tears. He felt himself drowning in her beauty, flaming against her gentle loving warmth. Then he lost all sense of caution and clutched her tightly in a spasm of uncontrolled desire.

His Julia had come back to him at last.

She felt his cheek, and it was wet with his tears. Softly, gently, she began to kiss them away.

*   *   *   *   *

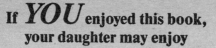

CHILDREN OF DESTINY

A trilogy by Ann Major

Three power-packed tales of irresistible passion
and undeniable fate created by Ann Major to
wrap your heart in a legacy of love.

PASSION'S CHILD — September

Years ago, Nick Browning nearly destroyed
Amy's life, but now that the child of his
passion—the child of her heart—was in danger,
Nick was the only one she could trust....

DESTINY'S CHILD — October

Cattle baron Jeb Jackson thought he owned
everything and everyone on his ranch, but fiery
Megan MacKay's destiny was to prove him wrong!

NIGHT CHILD — November

When little Julia Jackson was kidnapped, young
Kirk MacKay blamed himself. Twenty years later,
he found her ... and discovered that love could
shine through even the darkest of nights.

Silhouette Desire

COMING NEXT MONTH

#463 LADY OF THE ISLAND—Jennifer Greene
Getting involved with Jarl Hendricks was far too dangerous for fugitive Sara Chapman. She was trying to protect her child, and Jarl was the one man who could uncover her secret.

#464 A TOUCH OF SPRING—Annette Broadrick
Accompanying Colonel Alexander Sloan across the country on a promotional book tour started out as a routine assignment for publicist Stephanie Benson. But there was nothing routine about Alex!

#465 CABIN FEVER—Terry Lawrence
Trapped after an avalanche, her only contact the gruff voice of "Rescue Central," Autumn Kierney couldn't help fantasizing about the man. And reality more than met her expectations....

#466 BIG SKY COUNTRY—Jackie Merritt
When Slade Dawson decided to seduce his father's widow for revenge, he hadn't counted on falling in love with Tracy Moorland...or finding out who his real father was.

#467 SOUTHERN COMFORT—Sara Chance
Partners Victoria Wynne and Cord Darcourte were a professional team and the best of friends. But lately Victoria had been having very *unfriendly* thoughts about Cord!

#468 'TIS THE SEASON—Noreen Brownlie
Volunteering to bring Christmas cheer to an elderly person hadn't prepared Holly Peterson for fellow volunteer Nick Petrovich. Nick wanted much more than a fleeting holiday enchantment.

AVAILABLE NOW:

FOUR UNIQUE SERIES
FOR EVERY WOMAN YOU ARE . .

Silhouette Romance

Love, at its most tender, provocative, emotional . . . in stories that will make you laugh and cry while bringing you the magic of falling in love.

6 titles per month

Silhouette Special Edition

Sophisticated, substantial and packed with emotion, these powerful novels of life and love will capture your imagination and steal your heart.

6 titles per month

Silhouette Desire

Open the door to romance and passion. Humorous, emotional, compelling—yet always a believable and sensuous story—Silhouette Desire never fails to deliver on the promise of love.

6 titles per month

Silhouette Intimate Moments

Enter a world of excitement, of romance heightened by suspense, adventure and the passions every woman dreams of. Let us sweep you away.

4 titles per month

SILG-1R